FLIP SIDE OF
YESTERDAY

Recent Titles by Barbara Delinsky from Severn House

AN IRRESISTIBLE IMPULSE
MOMENT TO MOMENT
SWEET EMBER
A TIME TO LOVE
VARIATION ON A THEME

FLIP SIDE OF YESTERDAY

Barbara Delinsky

This title first published in Great Britain 2001 by
SEVERN HOUSE PUBLISHERS LTD of
9–15 High Street, Sutton, Surrey SM1 1DF.
This first hardcover edition published in the USA 2001 by
SEVERN HOUSE PUBLISHERS INC., of
595 Madison Avenue, New York, NY 10022,
by arrangement with HarperCollins*Publishers*, Inc.
Originally published in paperback format only 1983 in the
U.S.A. by Silhouette Books.

British Library Cataloguing in Publication Data

Delinsky, Barbara, 1945-
    Flip side of yesterday
    1.   Love stories
    I.   Title
    813.5'4 [F]

    ISBN 0-7278-5734-7

Printed and bound in Great Britain by
MPG Books Ltd., Bodmin, Cornwall.

Flip Side
of Yesterday

1

The evening breeze was gentle, softly whispering "Chl ... ooo ... eeeee ..." as the long-legged vision in white whisked across the dusky lawn, her dark hair streaming behind her, and ran lithely up the broad stone steps.

"Chloe! There you are. I was beginning to worry." A man stepped from beneath the deep brick overhang and fell into easy step beside her as they passed through a large oak door into the high school and headed down a long corridor.

"I'm sorry, Howard," she said, meaning it. Howard Wolschinski was the state senator who had first sought her services. After three meetings, she had come to like him. "I'd hoped to be on the road by four, but, I swear, there was a conspiracy against me. First the phone, then my car."

"Anything major with either?" he asked.

"No on both counts. But I didn't clear Little Compton until five, and by that time the rush-hour traffic was horrid. I drove as fast as I could. I hope I haven't messed things up."

"You haven't. The meeting was called for seven thirty. You're only five minutes late. It's given the crowd a chance to settle down." He guided her around a corner with a light hand at her elbow and began the climb as soon as they reached a staircase.

At the first landing, Chloe asked, "How's the turnout?"

He grinned sheepishly. "I only wish we did half as well at political rallies. This is a welcome change from apathy. The auditorium is packed. There must be several hundred people in there."

Chloe was surprised and decidedly pleased. "Several hundred? Not bad for a county meeting in New Hampshire." She smiled, lowering her voice dramatically. "But which side are they on? Are they for us or agin' us?"

Her humor drifted unanswered into the stale schoolhouse air as Howard ushered her into the meeting hall, led her onto the stage, and gestured her into a seat. He took one by her side. As though on cue, the crowd silenced and the moderator began.

"Ladies and gentlemen," he said in a voice made flat by its broad New England slant, "on behalf of my friends and, uh"—he cast an encompassing glance backward, then turned a cough into a

snicker, bringing chuckles from the audience—
"adversaries here on the stage with me, I would
like to thank you for coming tonight. It's a rare
pleasure to see so many of you gathered at once.
We realized that the issue of the Rye Beach Resort
and Condominium Complex would stir a few of
you to action, but we had no idea how many. I
don't believe we've had a response like this since
that talk of a state prison here a while back."

Chloe was wondering who the man was when
Howard whispered, "He's Felix Hart—town manager, commissioner of public safety, President of
the United States in his dreams."

She smiled at the quip. Nodding her thanks for
the information, she refocused on the speaker.

". . . and they listened to us then, just as they listened to us when they mentioned a hazardous
waste disposal center six miles from us. And before
that, there was the matter of a state sales tax . . ."

The monologue went on, freeing Chloe for several seconds more. Bending forward, she drew a
notebook from her bag and prepared to make
notes on the opposition's points. That opposition
sat to her left, occupying two chairs on the far side
of the one vacated by the moderator. Her periph-
eral vision took in two men, one significantly
taller and darker than the other. They would be
the state representative in favor of the complex
and the owner of the development company.

Chloe knew neither of their names, a situation that was about to be remedied.

"As for the others here tonight," the moderator said, "let me begin with Howard Wolschinsky. You all know Howard, our distinguished state senator." He gestured from Howard to Chloe. "Chloe MacDaniel, geological consultant and one of the founding partners of Earth Science Education, Inc., out of Little Compton, Rhode Island." His hand went toward the other side of the stage. "Bradbury Huff, your state representative"—she jotted the name in her notebook—"and finally, the president of the Hansen Corporation, Ross Stephenson . . ." R-O-S-S S-T-E—

Chloe stopped writing mid-stroke. Ross Stephenson? Ross Stephenson? She would never forget that name. Heart pounding, she glanced at the fourth member of the panel. He was the taller, darker one. Was it the same Ross Stephenson? This man was nattily dressed and impeccably groomed. The Ross she had known had been bearded and wore faded jeans, high boots, and a peasant shirt of Indian cotton. Eleven years had passed. He might have changed. How could she know?

His eyes. They were the same memorable amber. Eleven years ago they had cut through all pretense and snagged her in the space of a breath. They were just as striking now—and they were looking at her. He knew.

As all else faded, she felt shock, remembrance, pain. Then she tore her eyes from his and lowered them to her paper. P-H-E-N-S-O-N. Ross Stephenson. Un-believable.

"Are you all right?" Howard whispered, seeming to sense her distress.

She contemplated lying. The society belle of New Orleans would have done that. But today's Chloe was too honest. She whispered back, "I knew him—Ross—a long time ago. I never expected to see him here." Or again, for that matter, she added silently, struggling to keep her thoughts from racing back in time.

"He shakes you up?"

She smiled ruefully. "He shakes me up."

"Will you be able to go on and speak?"

She took a deep breath. "I'll be fine once we get going." Unfortunately, Felix Hart continued to talk, gesticulating more emphatically than ever.

"He's been sidetracked on the background of your pal. Listen."

Chloe had no choice.

"As many of you know," Felix drawled with an air of self-importance, "Mr. Stephenson has been behind the building of two successful mall complexes here in the Granite State. His company has left its mark from coast to coast in factories, libraries, educational facilities, and office buildings. The reputation of the Hansen Corporation precedes him here. It is with great honor that I present to you, for an explanation of his plans and hopes for the Rye Beach Complex, Mr. Ross Stephenson."

Chloe's heart was hammering again. When it was momentarily drowned out by the applause of the crowd, she dared another glance at Ross. Again, he was looking at her. She held her breath, barraged by memories that gathered and surged. A slow pallor spread beneath her ivory skin. She was thinking that she had to get out of there fast, when he finally faced forward, pushed himself from his chair, and approached the dais.

"Whew," came a whisper by her ear. "That was some greeting."

Chloe felt the color rush back to her face. She realized her misunderstanding when Howard went on. "Felix introduced him like he was a visiting dignitary instead of the man whose blueprints we plan to tear apart."

"Please keep reminding me," Chloe murmured, to which the senator chuckled. Then they both settled back to listen to Ross Stephenson's presentation.

For Chloe, listening was an awesome challenge. The sight of him standing straight and tall before the microphone was a distraction in and of itself. She couldn't help but admire the breadth of his shoulders and the slow tapering of his frame toward narrow hips and long, lean legs. To her chagrin, she couldn't help but remember the skin beneath, firm and drawn taut over the muscles of shoulder, chest, and arms, its dark matting of hair a cushion for her head, a playground for her fingers.

She forced those fingers to work now, making notes of words that she barely heard, that her mind could barely assimilate. Still she made herself concentrate, jotting down thoughts with increasing rapidity in an attempt to keep her mind on the present and off the past.

But was it the past that brought her head up again and her gaze back to Ross? Was she intrigued for old times' sake alone? His dark hair was thick but well-trimmed and combed into as much submission as she guessed it would go. Eleven years ago it had been longer and even thicker. With the beard, he was like a bear—large, overpowering, dominant, but cuddly. Now there was a refinement to him, a control in his stance, a purposefulness. Addressing his audience, he conveyed competence and intelligence.

And that audience was enrapt, some nodding, others shaking their heads, all measuring his words with the keen interest that had brought them out on this mild September night.

His voice was deep and resonant as it flowed through the mike and filled the room. "The benefit to your community would be multifold. We're proposing to use a parcel of land that is presently underused. The resort will attract guests who will patronize local businesses. Food outlets, entertainment houses, restaurants, real estate establishments—all stand to gain from the Rye Beach Complex. The condominium complex will bring untold tax revenue both to state and local purses. Given the easy access to this area by the federal highway system, the condominium units will be in high demand year round."

Chloe found herself listening closely, wondering how this could be the same man who had once chosen to live on a communal farm in Kentucky. That free-spirited Ross was a far cry from this entrepreneurial one. Trying to reconcile the two was impossible.

Howard leaned close. "He's a powerful speaker. What do you think? Will he have them sold before we even present our side?"

She answered without taking her eyes from Ross. "Lord, I hope not. I often work with groups of shoreline residents. They feel strongly about the land, which is their finest resource. I'll be appealing for the preservation of that resource."

"You're a powerful speaker yourself, Chloe. I heard you address that group on Martha's Vineyard on the subject of natural erosion patterns. You had them eating out of the palm of your hand."

Chloe gave a crooked smile. "Many of the issues are the same here. Let's hope they buy it, too."

Ross finished his formal presentation and opened the floor for questions. A podium and microphone had been set up in the center aisle of the auditorium. One by one, those residents with questions came forward. Most asked about specifics, all of which Chloe noted on her pad: the price range of the condominiums and the subsequent tax revenue; the time projection for the erection of the units; the capacity of the resort complex; and a listing of its self-contained facilities. At length, Felix Hart stood and joined Ross at center stage.

"I'm afraid we have to move on now," he apologized, eyeing the large clock on the front face of the balcony. "There's still another side to consider. Thank you, Mr. Stephenson. You've been very direct and a great help. Perhaps we'll have time for more questions later."

Chloe watched with growing excitement as Ross returned to his seat—and that excitement, for the moment, had nothing to do with him. She liked talking to groups like this, and did it often. Though she loved the scientific end of her job—the sample-taking and analysis, the computer work, the intricate calculations of ground composition, weather-related components, time predictions—she found the presentation of her findings to be heady.

Felix Hart made the introduction. "I have the delightful task now of giving you Ms. Chloe Mac-Daniel. Ms. MacDaniel has been retained by the county to study our coast with an eye toward the environmental impact of the Rye Beach Resort and Condominium Complex as proposed by the Hansen Corporation. She has already spent a good deal of time on the project. Ms. MacDaniel?"

After lifting a neat folder from the floor beneath her chair, Chloe rose to her full five-foot-eight-inch height and approached the podium. Her appearance was understated; she worked at that. Still, the curiosity of the crowd yielded to a murmur of appreciation when she stepped forward. Tall and willowy, dark haired and light complected, she was the image of grace. Her dress was of a soft and simple white eyelet fabric, lined through the bodice and skirt, the sleeves hanging free and loose to her elbows. A wide sash of contrasting aqua enhanced both the slimness of her waist and the porcelain of her skin.

Her voice was steady and well-modulated. "Thank you, Mr. Hart, for your kind introduction. Let me say how pleased I was to have been approached by your representatives last spring. Not only do I have a professional interest in your coastline, but I have an emotional involvement with the entire New England coast, since it's my home of choice. In keeping with this, let me begin by saying that I am not opposed to the Rye Beach Resort and Condominium Complex per se. What Mr. Stephenson has outlined for you sounds like a project that could benefit this area. But I question the ecological wisdom of the plan as it stands. The thought of a beachfront condominium may appeal to the romantic in us all, but this plan isn't environmentally wise."

As she proceeded to explain the core results of her tests, she was oblivious to all else but her work. The most powerful tool she had was genuine concern. "In terms of storm surge alone, the Hansen proposal is risky," she argued, pointing to the carefully calculated figures now projected on a slide screen. "Once every six or seven years you folks get a storm strong enough to do significant damage to structures built so close to the beach. If the entire complex were to be moved back an additional two hundred feet, the risk would be lessened."

Again she explained her theory in detail, using statistics where applicable. By the time she finished and opened the floor to questions, she felt that her arguments had been well received. She answered the questions posed with the same patience and care, the same genuine concern for the environment.

"Great presentation," Howard said when she returned to her seat.

She smiled modestly. "I only hope I've accomplished our objective. What happens now?"

"You endure brief speeches by Brad and myself. Try to stay awake."

She gave an of-course-I-will chuckle, but with her own job done, her mind wandered. While Felix introduced Bradbury Huff, she glanced at Ross. Folded comfortably into his seat, he appeared to be listening intently to his advocate, the state representative.

The years had been kind to Ross. While his dark brown hair had a touch of gray at the sideburns, it fell over his forehead with vibrance and class. There was strength in his unbearded jaw, which flexed as he listened. The crow's feet at the corners of his eyes were etched into a light tan that spoke of a life of sun and smiles. He was perfectly at ease, maddeningly confident, and devastatingly handsome.

He blinked once, turned his head, and met her gaze and, in that instant, time stopped. In the next, it reversed, speeding Chloe back over the years to the first time she'd seen him. It had been a beautiful Thanksgiving night in New Orleans, the moment as clear to her as if it had been yesterday. She had been with Crystal then. Crystal. She still missed her sister with the kind of pain that ate at a person from the inside out.

Howard covered her tight fist with his hand. "Are you all right?" He followed her line of sight. "You can talk with him later—"

"No," she interrupted, "no need." Embarrassed, she leaned toward Howard. "I'm sorry. There are . . . memories."

"There must be," he noted softly. "And from the looks of you, they're pretty awful."

It was a minute before she said, "Not all."

"You're white as a sheet. Can I get you some water or something?"

"No. I'm fine." At his quirked brow she added, "Really," before glancing at the podium. "Is Huff almost done?"

"He'd better be. I'm next. Take notes for me, will you? I have a tendency to forget what I say from one minute to the next."

"Baloney."

"Hmmm, I could use some of that, too. Supper was very early. It's nearly ten."

At least he'd had supper. She hadn't eaten a thing. "How much longer do you think this will last?" She still had to make the return trip to Little Compton that night.

Howard checked his watch. "I have no idea. But I have to be out of here by ten-thirty to make it to Manchester for the eleven o'clock news. They're doing a live interview. I hope good old Brad speeds it up."

He got his wish within minutes. As Chloe sat back, the long-winded state representative transferred the podium to "my illustrious colleague in the New Hampshire state government," and Howard took the reins.

Chloe did take notes. It was the one way she could keep her thoughts in the present and her eyes away from Ross. Once upon a time, he had played a cataclysmic role in her life. So much had happened since that night.

When Howard finished delivering a poignant plea for the preservation of the coast, the crowd came alive with questions and comments that had less to do with scientific matters, than practical ones. They wanted to know things like how increased tax revenues would be used to benefit local residents, and who would pay for the added police and fire coverage that would be necessary, given the proportions of the Rye Beach proposal.

It was closer to ten-forty before Howard was allowed to leave the microphone. To Chloe, with a frantic look at the time, he said, "Thanks again, Chloe. Think you can cover for me here a few minutes longer?"

"Sure thing, if I can answer their questions. My field is geology, not politics."

"Don't underestimate yourself. Why not change your mind and spend the night? There are a number of nice inns close by. It'll be a long drive back to Rhode Island alone."

She was touched by his worry, but confident. "I'll be fine. Driving relaxes me. I have plenty of unwinding to do." A movement in the corner of her eye reminded her of the source of her tension. She ignored the tall figure who approached for all she was worth. "Go on now, Senator. You'll be late."

Howard's expression was wry. "I already am. Take care." He shot a glance at Ross. "Let me know what happens."

Chloe found no humor in his double meaning, particularly with Ross suddenly at her side. "I think they'd like to ask us a few more questions," he said and she suddenly wished Howard had stayed, if only to serve as a buffer. She was on her own now.

With a forced smile, she stood. "Fine," was all she was able to murmur as she walked to the podium.

Luck was with her. The questions from the audience came quickly, reimmersing her into the world of coastal geology. She parried the on-slaught with ease, rising to meet the challenge in spite of an unease in the pit of her stomach. It was only when a question was directed at Ross that she let herself look at him again. The breadth of his shoulders was more marked now that his jacket was open and pulled back by the hand in his trousers' pocket. His other hand rested on the podium, fingers long and straight, tanned, relaxed.

Several questions later, a gruff-looking local came forward. "I have a question for Ms. Mac-Daniel," he said in a forceful voice. It brought her mind back, along with a certain wariness. "Yes?"

He stared straight at her. "I want to know what makes you qualified to be a consultant. You look awful young and awful pretty." His words took on a faint sneer. "What's with you and Wolschinski? Are you a regular on his payroll?"

A murmur of dismay passed through the audience. It was small solace for the shock Chloe felt. In the past she'd had to defend her qualifications on occasion, but never in the wake of such a crude insinuation.

Poise and professionalism were called for, and she mustered them up. But when she opened her mouth to speak, Ross beat her to the mike.

"I believe," he said in a hard voice, "that your question has no relevance—"

"Excuse me for interrupting, Mr. Stephenson." She leaned toward the mike, looking at Ross for the first time entirely in the context of the present. "I would like to respond to the gentleman." Her expression brooked no argument. She was determined. Ross straightened and backed off, seeming bemused.

She looked back at the man in the audience. "First things first, Mr.—"

"—Younger," he supplied, dropping the *r* at the end of his name in true New England form.

"—Mr. Younger. I have a bachelor of science in geology from Williams College in Williamstown,

Massachusetts, and a master's in geology from Boston College. I spent three years working for ConAm Petroleum, performing geological studies on oil deposits in the Gulf of Mexico. I was then able to co-found Earth Science Education, Inc., the consulting firm that was contacted by Senator Wolschinski to study the pros and cons of the Rye Beach Resort and Condominium Complex." Holding the man's gaze steadily, she pushed on. "I have control over neither my age nor my looks. And I never worked for Senator Wolschinski prior to the day he retained my services for this project." She tipped up her chin a hair. "Have you any other questions?"

Again a collective murmur went through the crowd. Just as the man shrugged and stepped back, Chloe saw the hand on the podium lift. Ross pressed his chin with his thumb, looking satisfied, respectful.

He wasn't the only one she had impressed. A different voice rose from the audience. "The taxpayers' money has been well spent for a change. Thank you, Ms. MacDaniel!"

Chloe directed a full smile across the ocean of heads as she leaned toward the microphone a final time. "It's been my honor. If my effort here has helped to preserve the natural bounty of your state, then we've all benefited. Thank you."

It was the perfect time to make a gracious, if

not sweeping exit. With Ross still standing aside in deference to the crowd applauding its appreciation of her, she should have quit while she was ahead. Her mistake was in looking back at him.

His smile was devastating. Chloe felt her chest tighten, as she was caught in the throes of memory again. She was suddenly immobilized, suspended in a matrix of desire and guilt that canceled out the years that had come between, until there was only yesterday, Ross, Crystal, and the toss of a coin.

When a last-minute surge brought members of the audience to the stage, a shaken Chloe returned to the present. She had to concentrate again, listening to questions, offering answers. She stood at one side of the stage with her followers, Ross stood at the other side with his. She gained strength with each new question, so that when the last of the locals left, she felt more herself—felt more herself, that is, until she realized that she and Ross were alone.

He showed no sign of sharing either her awkwardness or her apprehension. Rather, he smiled at her, looking older and wiser perhaps, but no less alive. The air between them hummed, just as it had eleven years before.

Looking at him, Chloe grappled with a world of inner demons, but the past was better left alone. She was determined to make this reunion as brief as possible.

"How are you, Chloe?" he asked, crossing the stage to where she stood.

He was that much taller than she was. She had to tip up her head. "Fine. And you?"

"Not bad. You're looking well." He gave her a warm once-over. "Very different." Humor tugged at the corners of his lips.

"So are you." Even in spite of an inner trembling, she could appreciate the humor. "When I last saw you, you were distinctly antiestablishment. This is a switch."

His stance was a casual one, the hand in his pocket not only emphasizing the solid wall of his chest but pulling the fabric of his trousers across his thigh in a way that showed the strength of seemingly endless legs.

"Not entirely. It's just that now I save my jeans for free-time wear and my boots for cold weather."

So he, too, remembered what he had worn that night. "And the peasant shirt?" she asked softly.

He laughed. "The peasant shirt was replaced for a while by a dashiki, but I'm afraid the modern me is addicted to ordinary sports shirts and sweaters."

"Conventional," she murmured with a faltering smile, teasing him as much as she dared. It was hard to remain indifferent to this man. She felt the strain.

"Sadly so," he agreed without any sadness. "But look at you. You've done a turnaround. Last time I saw you, your hair was curled, you wore makeup, higher heels, and more daring clothes. You also talked New Orleans. Where'd the accent go?"

Chloe drew in a long breath. "It faded. I've lived up north for too long. Time does different things to each of us, I guess."

"It's for the better. You look beautiful. Unhappy, but beautiful."

His candor made her balk. Seeing him was painful enough. Talking more with him could be a total trauma.

She glanced at the auditorium clock. "My Lord, it's nearly twelve. I have to run." Straightening the shoulder strap of her pocketbook and hugging the large folder to her breast, she went to the stage steps. Ross followed. Under the guise of worry at the lateness of the hour, she quickened her step. He kept stride easily.

"You're not driving back tonight, are you?"

"I am."

"All the way to . . . ?"

"Little Compton."

"That has to be a good two- to three-hour drive. Wouldn't you do better to get an early start in the morning?"

"Can't do. I have an early appointment in the morning." Her voice sounded breathy. It was the rush, she told herself.

For long moments, Ross said nothing. They

reached the front door. He held it; she passed through. In silence they crossed the lawn that separated the high school from the parking lot.

"I admire you, Chloe," he said, sounding sincere. "Your work is interesting. You obviously enjoy it."

"I do," she agreed. Relieved to be at her car, she fished in her purse for her keys. The sooner she was back at that work, back in the security of her seafront home, the sooner she could turn the past off again. Slipping in behind the wheel, she rolled her window down to let in the cool night air. With escape imminent, she grew bolder, looking up at Ross as he leaned over with his fingers curved on the lowered window. How handsome he was, she mused. She had been powerfully attracted to him then; she still was. "It was nice seeing you, Ross."

"You won't change your mind and stay over? I'm at the Wayward Sailor, an inn just down the road. I'm sure they have another vacancy, since the height of the season is past. We could grab a snack somewhere and talk."

Chloe would have liked nothing better. She knew nothing about the Ross Stephenson who was a successful businessman. Instinct told her that time spent with him would be interesting. It would also be downright dangerous, even devastating.

She sighed. "That would be nice, but I have to

get back. I feel wide awake for driving. I'd just as soon put the miles behind me. Besides, I have that appointment."

Ross considered that for a minute, then held up his hands. In gracious defeat, he stepped back. She put the key in the ignition, pumped the gas pedal, turned the key. There was a click, but nothing happened. She repeated the sequence. It always worked. Granted, her small blue compact had seen better days, but it had always started for her—until, she realized as she turned the key a third time, this afternoon. She had heard the same click then, had run back into the house and brought Lee out to help. They had figured the engine was flooded, had waited and won. The car had started. But Murphy's Law said that it wasn't going to start now.

"Trouble?" Ross bent in at the window again.

"Battery, I think."

He opened the door. "Let me try."

She slid out. With an ease that belied his awesome length, he folded himself behind the wheel. The front seat was already back to allow for the length of Chloe's own long legs, and even then he gave a good-natured grimace. She had to smile. Getting in was apparently the easy part. Maneuvering now that he was there was the challenge.

But he managed. When he tried the ignition, though, he had no better luck than Chloe. He listened to that impotent click once, twice, three times. Then he hoisted himself out of the car and looked under the hood.

"You're right," he said, straightening. "It's the battery." He slammed the hood shut and brushed his palms against one another. "It looks like you'll have to stay. I don't see how you'll get someone to come out at this hour."

She reached for her bag. "I have triple-A."

"Chloe." He sighed softly. "This isn't a bustling metropolis. By the time—"

"Do you have jumper cables?"

"No." He patted his pockets. "Not anywhere close by."

"In your car?"

"It's a rental."

Her gaze fell to the pavement. She could rant and rave all she wanted, but it seemed she had little choice. "I suppose Lee could change that early appointment for me," she murmured quietly, then looked up. "And you think your inn would have a room?"

His gaze was steady. "I'm sure it would."

Not one to belabor a no-win situation, Chloe sighed. "Lead on, Ross. Lead on."

2

Ross led her to a late-model rental car roomy enough for both pairs of long legs to stretch comfortably. Vibes were something else. Chloe sensed that no space would be large enough for the ones that circuited back and forth during the short drive to the inn.

"You flew in just for tonight's meeting?" she asked, seeking to ease the silence. It was awkward, given the intimacy they had once shared.

"That's right," he answered, paying close attention to roads that were now dark and deserted.

"From?"

"New York."

"Do you live there?"

"Occasionally."

It was an odd answer. When he failed to elaborate, Chloe tried again. "Have you had to come here often?"

"More often than I'd anticipated. This project has created something of a stir." If the glance he shot her was accusatory, she accepted it as fair game and took no offense. She believed in her cause.

"From what Felix Hart implied, you move around a lot," she said.

"I always did."

It was a direct reference to the past. Then, he had been in the Peace Corps on leave for Thanksgiving, the world traveler coming stateside for a visit. There had been an air of excitement about him.

He still had it. His profile was strong, lean, preoccupied in ways that suggested big business in far places. She looked away, focusing on the view outside her window, trying to ignore a silence that she could feel and taste. She was relieved when the Wayward Sailor came into view.

Ross turned to her as soon as the car stopped. His features had softened. His tone was solicitous. "Why don't you wait here? I'll make the arrangements and find out where we can get a bite to eat. You are hungry, aren't you?"

She smiled awkwardly. "I haven't had anything since lunch."

"No wonder you're pale." He touched her cheek. "Stay put. I'll be right back."

She sat quietly, trying to think of anything but Ross. Just when she was on the verge of declaring defeat, he loped back down the steps of the charmingly ancient house. "Any luck?" she asked when he reached the car.

"There's good news and bad news." He was leaning down to talk through the window again.

"Give me the good news first," Chloe said. She needed that, needed it bad.

He grinned. "The good news is that you have the penthouse."

She looked up the inn's façade to the very top, the third floor. Assuming the attic was clean and had a bed, it would do. "The penthouse is fine." She scrunched up her face. "What's the bad news?"

He opened the door with a flourish. "The bad news is that no one serves food at this hour. The night manager here says we can raid his refrigerator, though." He paused, staring down at her for a minute before offering his hand to help her out. "The service won't be fancy. We'll be on our own." The warning note in his voice jarred her. He was remembering the old Chloe. That Chloe had been spoiled. She hadn't known how to cook, having had everything done for her for the entire eighteen years of her life. But her lifestyle had changed drastically since then.

She rose from the car. "That's fine. I think we can manage." Oh, yes, she could certainly manage to put together a meal. She was actually a fine cook now. But it occurred to her that she and Ross would be alone. She wasn't so sure about managing that.

A frown creased her brow as she entered the inn with Ross by her side. He left his overnight case at the front desk with the night manager, who cheerfully directed them into the kitchen, a decidedly old room into which every modern convenience had been crammed. Chloe made herself at home. Only after she had placed a crock of steaming beef stew, put together from leftovers, and a half-loaf of what appeared to be home-baked bread on the table did she realize that she had done all the work. But it had kept her mind occupied. Ross had been in and out of the room as she worked, finally settling down on a tall stool by a butcher-block counter to watch.

His presence didn't upset her now as much as it had earlier. She had gotten over the shock, she guessed. Still, she felt vaguely shy when they were actually ready to eat.

"Uh, is there anything else you want?" She skimmed the simple place settings, the two large bowls filled with stew. "A drink?"

He made no move to help himself. For old times' sake, so the liberated woman told herself, she indulged him.

"Milk would be fine."

He waited while she searched for glasses and filled two. She sat down opposite him. Once several mouthfuls of the thick stew had warmed her stomach, she put her spoon down. Something stuck in her craw.

"I'm not unhappy," she stated, so softly and apparently unexpectedly that Ross looked perplexed. "You thought I looked unhappy. I'm not."

He went back to eating, but slowly, thoughtfully. "No, I suppose you're not, not right now," he finally said. "But earlier, there was a look in your eyes. It comes and goes. There it is again."

The sound of his voice had been enough to spark memories. With a barely perceptible shake of her head, she chased them off again. "I do love what I'm doing," she said.

"Tell me about it. How did you get started?"

"You heard the bare outline tonight."

"The bare outline. Now I'd like to hear more." His pause was pregnant with unspoken thoughts. "Why geology?"

She shrugged. "Why not?"

He didn't pull any punches. "Because it's one of the last fields that someone raised in the style of conspicuous consumption would choose."

"Maybe that's why I chose it."

"Ah." He smiled. "You were rebelling."

"Not entirely."

"Escaping?"

She looked away. "You're perceptive. But only half right."

"Go on."

Chloe tucked a long strand of dark hair behind her ear. "It was actually a simultaneous discovery—escape and excitement. At that period of my life, I needed something that was a total change from everything I'd known before. I spent some time in Newport with friends and fell in love with the ocean there."

"You found solace?" he asked gently.

She admitted it with a small tilt of her head. "I spent a lot of time on the beach and happened to befriend an old man who felt very strongly about environmental considerations. He affected me deeply." The memory of Hector Wallaby brought a sad smile to her lips.

"He's dead?"

"Yes. I miss him. He never knew it, but in spirit at least, he was the founding father of ESE, Inc."

"Were you in college during the time you knew him?"

Chloe sat straighter. "Uh, no. I . . . my freshman year was postponed."

"So you started college late and have still done all this?"

The compliment gave her a boost. She smiled. "Once I decided to go into geology I was in a rush."

Ross smiled back. Firm lips framed the whitest of teeth, mesmerizing her for the split second until he said, "You worked for ConAm Petroleum?"

"Yes. Do you know the company?"

He shook his head. "Only by reputation." He looked at her sideways, skeptical now. "I'd have thought that if environmental concerns were your focus, the oil companies would be your archenemies."

She blushed. He made nothing easy, that was for sure. But if he wanted to be honest, she could be honest right back. "I needed the money," she said and braced herself for the response that was sure to come.

And she wasn't let down. Ross's eyes widened, then narrowed. "You needed the money?" He frowned. "Did I miss something here? I was given to think James MacDaniel was—is—one of the wealthiest men in New Orleans."

"He is."

"Then, why . . . ?"

"Among other things," she began in self-defense, "it was a matter of pride. I wanted to start my own consulting firm and didn't want to ask my father for money." Ross should know how much she had changed. He should know that she was her own woman now.

But his take on the situation was different from hers. "So you sold out to the powers that be for the amount of time it took you to gather the resources to mount a systematic campaign against those same powers?"

Chloe reacted quickly and vehemently. "That's not true. Not true at all. The work I did for the oil companies involved identifying the most likely spots for oil deposits. Wherever possible, environmental considerations were put first. And you're a fine one to talk about selling out. I had the impression, when I saw you last, that you were against everything the establishment had to offer."

Ross leaned back in his chair. "You drew your own conclusions, Chloe. Appearances can be misleading." His tone was low, his voice and eyes steady.

Chloe was stunned. She stood up and cried, "It was all a charade, then? The clothes, the beard, even the Peace Corps?" She turned away, disillusioned and heartsick. Head bowed, she grappled with the idea of an attraction based on a lie.

Ross materialized before her. "Did it matter so much?" he asked softly. When she neither answered nor looked up, he put a finger under her chin and forced it up. Her eyes were dry, but she knew they held pain. She couldn't hide that, couldn't even try.

"Did it?" he asked.

Chloe felt a well of emotion, emotion that had lain dormant for years. Ross was so close that the warmth of his body was an intoxicant. She used the power of that to speak. "Yes. It mattered more than you can imagine."

"But why? The physical attraction between us had nothing to do with outer trappings. As I recall, we shed our clothes pretty fast." Chloe tried to pull away, he held her chin. "Don't run from it. There was something between us that you can't deny. Are you telling me you made love to an image?" His tone was suddenly cooler. "Was it an experiment for you? Was I a tool in your rebellion?" His fingers tightened on her jaw. Reflexively, she held his wrist.

"No. That wasn't it at all." She was hurt that he would suggest it. "All you seem to think about is the physical act. Yes, there was a physical attraction. With and without clothes. But for me, at least, there was more involved. There had to be." Her voice rose. "I was a virgin, for God's sake."

Ross must have felt her hurt, because he relaxed his grip. He moved his fingers back to her ear, pushing them through the long strands of her hair with infinite gentleness.

"I know that," he whispered. His eyes held the same tenderness they had on that night, when he had first introduced her to the art of love. Then, the world had been hers on a string. It certainly wasn't now, still her heart pounded in her chest the very same way. Now, as then, she was being held by the most appealing man she had ever known. He was a leader, a freethinker. He was boldly gentle, gently bold. He had confidence without arrogance, success without acclaim. He was a man who didn't mince words. She felt an instinctive respect for him.

Much of this same appeal had beckoned to her on that night. Other details might be forgotten, but not Ross and the force that bound them. It was an unfathomable force, but frightfully powerful. Eleven years ago, it had driven the fact of her innocence from her mind. Now it obliterated all remembrance of what had happened so soon after that night to irrevocably change Chloe's life and outlook.

As Ross's large hands framed her face, she felt a special warmth steal through her, awakening senses from hibernation like the coming of spring. Her cheeks flushed with the heat. Her lips parted. She was entranced all over again.

He moved closer, his face lowering. When she closed her eyes it was to savor the feather touch of his mouth on hers. It seemed she had waited forever to know its sweetness again. And guilt? Guilt was light-years away, beyond a far horizon she hoped never to reach. It had been pervasive over the years, but was out of place now. She wanted more of Ross, if only to keep the past safely blotted from her mind.

Opening her eyes, she found Ross's hot above her. His breath was unsteady, but he waited. She sensed he was giving her a chance to turn and run, but that was the last thing she wanted to do.

She met his kiss with an eagerness she hadn't known for eleven years. All the power of her femininity that had been stored up and denied now burst forth. Ross's lips were firm and knowing in response to her passion, dominating then submitting, teasing then yielding. They explored the ripe curve of her mouth with a thoroughness surpassed only when his tongue entered the act. And Chloe opened herself more with each darting flicker, with each exchange of breath.

She had come alive and was aflame. At some point her arms found his neck and coiled beyond, drawing her slender body firmly against his longer, harder one. His hands played over her back, caressing every inch from hip to neck with the devastating touch of those long fingers. And she was caught in the web they spun, neither able nor willing to move away.

Everything about Ross was utterly male, from the musky scent of his skin to the trim tapering of the hair at the top of his collar, to the lean line of his torso and the corded steel of his thighs. It was as though Chloe was innocent again, as though this was that first ecstatic night relived. She was intoxicated.

When he groaned and crushed her to him, she understood the feeling. It was a statement of a shared primal need. Ross held something for her that no other man had begun to offer. She was driven by instinct closer, closer to him.

At some point, soft bells of warning sounded. She didn't know if it was when his hand slipped from her cheek to her throat, or when his fingers began to knead her breast, or when his palm turned to her nipple. She only knew of a tug between some relic of the past that clamored for recognition, and the quickly coiling knot of need deep inside.

She fought that past by nurturing the need. Hands locked at the back of his neck, she closed her eyes, let her head fall back, and sought the mindlessness of sensual pleasure. Her lips parted; her breathing was short. But she needed more. Against her better judgment, against those tiny warning bells, she grew bolder. Bowing her head, bracing it against his chin, she was curved now, offering him an entrance he hadn't had before.

Small explosions of delight flared through her when he slid his hand into her dress. Surrounded, her breast was warm, full, and straining against his hand. His thumb and forefinger met at a nipple, driving her higher. Did reason exist? At that instant she knew of only one road to satisfaction.

"Come upstairs with me," Ross said in a voice thick with need. "Let me love you. It's been so long, princess."

Princess. It struck her that he had done the same

thing she had—formed an image and held it through the years. In his mind she was still one step removed from royalty. But not in hers.

She strained away from his hands. "Please stop, I can't do this." Aroused still and upset with herself, she trembled.

"Can't?" he challenged hoarsely.

"Won't," she amended as she clutched at threads of composure. Eleven years ago she hadn't refused him. Her virginity had never had a chance. But things were different now. She was different.

"Why not, Chloe?"

She heard hurt, but it didn't make her relent. "I wish I could explain."

"Why can't you? I've seen that pained look in your eyes. At those moments—at this moment— you do look unhappy. Is it something about me? Something about what happened eleven years ago?"

For all of those eleven long years, Chloe had hidden a world of inner feelings from everyone around her. They were locked in tight. He could prod all he wanted, but they weren't getting out.

He spoke more gently. "Here. Sit down. I'll make us some coffee. You can talk."

"I don't want to talk. Some things are best left dead and buried." She shuddered at her own choice of words.

"Sit." He nudged her into the chair she had left,

and she sat, if only because her legs were unsteady. He proceeded to clear the table, rinse everything, and perk a small pot of coffee. She watched almost incidentally, her thoughts far off in a world of what-ifs. What if Crystal had won that toss of the coin? What if Crystal had set out to seduce Ross and been seduced herself? What if Crystal had died anyway? Would Chloe feel the same guilt now?

"How do you take it?" Ross asked, placing a steaming mug before her.

"Black. Thank you."

After lacing his own with milk and sugar, he returned to his seat.

Chloe tried to control her thoughts by speaking first. "You've come a long way in the business world since I saw you last, Ross. How did you manage it?"

He smiled. "You mean, how did I manage the transformation from 'far out' to 'far in'? The fact is, I never was all that 'far out.' I went my own way for a while. I avoided money. I grew a beard because there wasn't modern plumbing where I was in Africa, and I didn't want to have to shave at dawn by the riverside. I wore jeans because they were comfortable, same with loose shirts. I'd grown up in a world of rigid discipline. I wanted my freedom."

" 'Rigid discipline'?" She realized again how little she knew of Ross.

He eyed her with something akin to amusement. "Y'know, considering you slept with the man the first time you met him . . ."

"That's not fair," she argued. "When we were together, I couldn't think straight."

"History repeats itself," he drawled, referring to what had happened moments earlier with a mischievous grin.

Chloe didn't like being ribbed. "You didn't know any more about me that night." But rather than turning the tables, she was more deeply incriminated.

"Neither of us did much talking, did we?" Ross asked, clearly enjoying himself.

She shook her head. The only talking they'd done had been in soft moans and caresses. The attraction between them had been overpowering. "I want you to know that I don't do that as a rule. I mean, I don't make a habit of—"

"—jumping into bed with every guy that comes along? I know that, Chloe." He smiled gently. "I told you that we had something special. Do you think I sleep with every pretty woman I meet?"

"Of course not. I just wanted you to know not to expect something I can't give."

"Won't give," he corrected a second time.

"The end result is the same. You understand, don't you?"

"No, I hear you. I'm listening." He was sober.

"But I don't understand. You haven't given me a good reason to understand yet. Most women with your looks would have reached the point, at age twenty-nine, where they could recognize something deeper."

Chloe felt stymied. "What do my looks have to do with anything?"

The amber gaze that touched her curves gave the answer even before he spoke. "You're beautiful, Chloe. Beautiful women have options. You've never married?"

"No."

"You must date often."

"I have friends."

"Male friends?"

"Some."

"Serious male friends?"

When she shrugged, he looked at the ceiling. "What I'm trying to find out is whether you're going with someone, living with someone, or engaged to someone."

For an instant, Chloe imagined he was a frustrated suitor. She smiled at the thought. "No, Ross. I date here and there, but there's no one special. I live alone."

When he expelled a breath, she suspected it was for effect. "Thank you," he added facetiously, then sobered. "Do you go home much?"

Chloe flinched. "No." That was another topic

better left alone. "What about you? What was that 'rigid discipline' you suffered through?"

"My father was heart-and-soul Army. A career man. Our house was run like a barracks. It was almost a treat when I was sent to military school."

"Oh, my. It's no wonder you freaked out."

Ross laughed. "Freaked out? That's one from the old days."

Chloe smiled. "Sorry. It just slipped out. I can't remember the last time I said that."

"Maybe way back in the time of you and me?" He stared at her, then gazed pensively at the table. When he raised a hand and rubbed the muscles at the back of his neck, Chloe followed the movement. She half-wished she could do it for him, but dangerous was a mild word for that type of thing. Once, danger had been a challenge. Now she wanted no part of it.

Ross's confession broke into her thoughts. "I may have been pretty antiestablishment, at that. There was a certain amount of rebellion in me against routine and schedules and expectations. I guess I wasn't much different from the average flower child, except that I knew I'd be returning to the fold before long. I saw that period for what it was—a time in my life when I could stretch my legs."

Chloe chuckled. Her smoky gaze fell to the floor, where a pair of well-shod feet, ankles crossed, extended well beyond her side of the table. "An awesome task." She quirked a brow. "So how did you become a successful businessman? You obviously didn't go into partnership with your dad. But you've come a long way in eleven years. President of the Hansen Corporation." She shook her head in amazement.

"I had a mentor, like you did," he explained. "I worked for him through business school, then after. The business did well. I gradually acquired stock. When Sherman died two years ago he left me shares enough to make me the majority holder."

"Was the Rye Beach Complex your idea?"

"Actually, no. It was the baby of one of the other vice presidents. Sherman seemed to feel it had merit."

"And you don't?" Considering the force of his presentation that evening, she was startled.

"I do, with reservations."

"Why did you come up tonight then, rather than the VP who feels more strongly about it?"

Ross shrugged. "He's no longer with the corporation." He didn't look sorry. It struck Chloe that he might have fired the man, himself. She sensed his power. A free spirit, he had called himself. Now he ruled a prominent corporation. With an iron hand? Maybe. But he would use subtle methods to reach his goals.

"What do you plan to do about it?" she asked carefully.

"About what?"

"The complex. You mentioned some doubts. Tonight's meeting must have raised others. Will you change your proposal?"

"No."

"No? Building the complex as planned now would be environmentally dumb."

" 'Dumb'?" he mocked with a grin.

She felt put down with that one echoed word. Exasperated, she threw her hands in the air. "I gave all the reasons in that auditorium. I won't repeat them now. You're being bullheaded. Do you go about all your building projects this way?"

"What do you know about my building projects?" he asked with a trace of lingering amusement.

"Nothing. I had only heard of the Hansen Corporation before tonight. But if it's like most other businesses, it puts the dollar bill before every other consideration."

"Not always." His voice carried a warning now, but she sat straighter and barreled on.

"Then you acknowledge that profit is your raison d'être?"

To her chagrin, Ross laughed. "I would never be where I am today if I didn't have an eye out for profit!"

She felt oddly betrayed. "That's really pathetic," she said, recalling the tall, handsomely bearded man in jeans, boots, and a simple peasant shirt. "I'd have thought that, with what you stood for at one time, you might have minimized crass capitalism. You have sold out, which just goes to show how terribly wrong one person can be in the judging of another, or how naïve."

Ross had risen. His eyes were too dark to distinguish anger from hurt. "You don't know what you're talking about. You didn't know me then, and you certainly don't know me now. When I returned from Africa that last time with my grungy denims, my dashiki, and my beard"—his eyes narrowed—"it took me all of a week to shuck them. And do you know why?"

He went on only when she shook her head. "Because I saw that there was more narrow-mindedness, more prejudice, coming from the mouths of the hippie generation than anywhere else. Because of my appearance, I was assumed to be one of them, until they discovered that I didn't always think the way they did, that I had a mind of my own. The true sign of a liberal, Chloe, is accepting people for their differences, respecting their right to be different. Those others, the ones who prided themselves on being nonconformists, declared all-out war on the establishment. And what happened?"

Without waiting for her response he went on, his voice low but relentless, his gaze intense. He put his hands on the table. "When was the last time you saw a flower child? Hmm? They've vanished. Disbanded. Lost the war." The pause he took was for a deep breath. "Well, I haven't lost. I'm working from within to change things. Did that ever occur to you, Chloe? You've been so quick to label me first one way, then the other. Did it ever occur to you that your impression wasn't even skin deep, that there's a me under it all?"

It was a while before Chloe was able to speak. She certainly didn't know Ross. This speech presented a new side of him. And he was right.

"I'm sorry," she said. "It was wrong of me to do that. I'm not always that way." She tried a smile in apology. To her relief, it seemed to work. His features relaxed.

"Only with me, eh?" He inhaled deeply and stood tall, holding his breath for a minute while his head fell back, then releasing it as his eyes met hers.

She felt suitably contrite and suddenly drained. "You have a knack for bringing out my extremes. I guess I'm just tired. It's late." A glance at the bold face of Ross's watch told her exactly how late. "Oh, Lord! It's two in the morning!" She caught her breath, looked at the ceiling, and whispered, "Do you think we've woken anyone up?"

Ross's chiding was gentle. "No need to whisper

now. If our yelling didn't wake 'em, nothing will." He took the two empty coffee cups and brought them to the sink.

Chloe wiped off the table. "If it hadn't been for that battery, I'd have been back home in bed by now."

"Instead," he teased, "we've had a chance to get reacquainted. Um, acquainted."

Chloe stopped wiping and straightened. Getting acquainted was one thing, but where did they go from there? The physical attraction that had been rekindled with a vengeance earlier, weighed heavily on her now.

"Uh-uh, Chloe." He came up behind her. "Just relax." She looked back, wondering how he knew. "I can feel it in the air—that whatever-it-is that disturbs you." He took the cloth from her and tossed it into the sink. "I won't pounce. I'll just walk you to your room."

That was exactly what he did. He halted on the threshold. "The manager said he'd leave plenty of towels. I wish I could offer you something else. You seem to be without those . . . things that most women can't live without."

She smiled. "I don't need anything."

"A shirt? Would you like a fresh shirt of mine in place of a . . . a . . ."

"Negligee?" Her smile widened. "No, thanks, Ross. If the sheets are clean, they'll be covering enough. But I have to get an early start in the morning."

He nodded. "I called the garage while you were making our dinner. They'll be at your car no later than eight. Is that too early?"

"Lord, no! I have to call Lee, my partner, anyway. There's a small matter of an appointment at nine."

"Will she fill in for you?"

"No. He has work of his own to do." She grinned at Ross's startled look. "He'll cancel and explain for me. I'll reschedule when I get back."

Ross nodded, but he was gnawing on his lower lip. There was obviously more that he wanted to say, but Chloe wasn't inviting him in. That would be dangerous. Very dangerous. But when he turned and headed down the stairs to his own room, she felt disappointed. Part of her wondered if flirting with danger could end on a happy note this time.

The night manager hadn't only left extra towels, but he'd also left a package of goodies tailor-made for the stranded motorist. There was a tooth-brush, toothpaste, a comb, soap, and, luxury of luxuries, an envelope of bubble-bath powder.

Chloe smiled. She'd had her share of tension today; now she would release it. The devil could take the hour; she would take a long, hot bath! Several deft flicks of her wrist sent a full stream of hot water into the long porcelain tub, which stood, in keeping with the vintage aura of the inn itself, on four clawed feet. Feeling scandalous, she sprinkled the entire contents of the envelope beneath the steaming flow.

Moments later she was immersed to her neck in bubbles. Draping her hair over the lip of the tub, she closed her eyes and gave in to pleasure. Was it true what they said about the subconscious urge to return to the womb? Was this all-enveloping warmth, this light floating what it had been like?

The womb, however, was not where she wished most to be at that moment. Rather, she thought of the arms that had held her earlier, the lips that had kissed her, the strong body that had supported her. Buoyed by a sense of euphoria, she allowed herself to think back on the full story of that night eleven years ago.

It had been the holiday recess. She and Crystal had returned from their first semester at the university to spend Thanksgiving with the family. The boys were gathered: Allan from Denver, Chris from Chicago, Tim from St. Louis—from their respective subdivisions of the MacDaniel domain. They had spent a typically revel-filled Thanksgiving Day, complete with gargantuan offerings of turkey, stuffing, salads and vegetables and fruit molds, pies and cakes and other goodies, not to mention the company of aunts and uncles and cousins galore. Later that night, she and Crystal had dropped in at Sandra's house, where a party had been in progress.

Sandra had been their best friend through carefree high school years. They hadn't seen her since September when she had left to go to college in New York, where her older brother lived.

Ross was that brother's friend. From the moment Chloe set foot into the Brownings' living room her eye was drawn to him. He had seemed to represent all the things she had never known—nonconformity, independence, singularity. Even in a crowd, he stood out. Sandra had said he was in the Peace Corps, stationed in Africa. He was tall and breathtakingly attractive in a wholly new and exciting way for Chloe.

"Gorgeous, isn't he?" Crystal had whispered in the ear of her twin.

"I'll say. What do you think he's doing here?"

"That's a dumb question. He's visiting the Brownings like we are."

They stood with their heads together, both pairs of eyes glued to Ross. Chloe asked, "Do you think he has a girl?"

"A guy like that? Girls, plural. He's oozing virility—or hadn't you noticed?"

"I noticed," Chloe drawled. "Think he'll notice us?"

"Why not? We're rich and beautiful and sexy—"

"—and young."

Crystal bristled. "What's that got to do with anything?"

"If he's Sammy's friend, Crystal, he's ten years older than we are. You don't really think he'd be interested, do you?"

"God, Chloe, you are a stick-in-the-mud. Of course he'll be interested. Men like freshness. And we are rich and beauti—"

"I know, I know," Chloe interrupted the litany, feeling a sudden surprising disdain for her sister's arrogance. So often the arrogance was shared. As the babies of the family—and twins, at that— they'd been reared like royalty. For the first time, however, Chloe wondered whether men like this stranger were attracted to royalty. Was being rich and beautiful and sexy all that mattered? Something told her that this divine-looking man would seek more, something in his gaze as he slowly turned it their way.

"Wow," Crystal whispered. "I'm going after him."

"Oh, no. It's my turn," Chloe whispered back with matching determination. "You got Roger. This one's mine."

"He won't want a stick-in-the-mud. You think we're too young for him."

"I've changed my mind. Besides, he's looking at me, not you."

Crystal snorted. "Arbitrary choice. We look exactly alike."

"All of a sudden we look exactly alike?" Chloe choked. "What about that 'added bit of spice' you claim to have? What about your last-born 'glow of vulnerability'?"

Crystal crinkled her nose. "He can't see all that at this distance."

But Chloe was vehement. "I have a feeling about him."

"You always have feelings about people. I'm the doer. Remember?"

"Not this time."

"Chloe . . ." Crystal warned in a singsong murmur.

"Crystal . . ." Chloe warned right back. "We'll toss a coin. Heads, I win."

Crystal's eyes narrowed. "I'll do the tossing. You always seem to win."

It was true. While Crystal, with her heightened impishness and propensity for instigating trouble, was often at the fore in their mischief-making, Chloe invariably won the toss of the coin. And with good reason. As the more levelheaded of the two, she was expected to be the one to produce the coin. It came from a secret fold in her wallet and served no other purpose than this. It would never have passed for currency. It had two heads. But

Crystal never knew that, not even when she did the tossing herself.

And so, with the keenest of amber eyes pulling her forward, Chloe had approached the mysterious man of the love generation. Initial silence had given way to the exchange of smiles, then names. There was brief small talk, amid a riot of steamy looks. The party had paled. Forgetting their friends, they had wandered onto the patio, then taken refuge by the pool. Later they had moved on to the sloping lawn of Sandra's parents' estate.

Chloe shifted slowly in the tub. The heat of the water had dissipated, but was replaced by the heat of her body as she remembered. It had been warm that night. The crescent moon had been brilliant, repeated in the white smile that split Ross's dark beard when he looked down at her.

"You're a vision, Chloe," he whispered, sharing her fascination. "Are you real?"

"I'm real," she whispered back and was suddenly, uncharacteristically tongue-tied.

But further words were unnecessary. The guest house where Ross was staying was on a far corner of the estate. He took her there, pausing along the way to kiss her, to assure her with a protective embrace that he wouldn't hurt her, and he hadn't. He had been a masterful lover, so very gentle undressing her, so very subtle baring his potentially frightening body, so very patient as he coaxed her to heights of desire, then tender when he took her virginity. When tenderness gave way to driving passion, she rose with him, reveling in an ecstasy she had never known before.

Ross's lovemaking had been a magical experience. She would always cherish it.

She stirred in the tub, suspended between the world of memories and the present. In a final indulgence, she submerged her hand and touched the skin Ross had touched, traced the curves he had traced. Thoughts of him were fresh and near. She sighed in delight.

Then her back slipped on the porcelain. With a jerk, she sat up, but not before her hair got wet. Hissing her annoyance, she reached for a towel to wrap around her head, then soaped herself quickly and climbed out. A lovely trip into the past had ended in frustration. Satisfaction would not be forthcoming. Nor would there be a respite from the guilt she still felt.

For the guilt was only in part related to the act of loving Ross. Its other part was Crystal. Crystal—her twin. Crystal—her alter ego. Crystal—who had never known that same joy, but should have, should have at least once before her death such a short time later.

3

The long ponytail bobbed against her neck as Chloe jogged on the beach. Indian summer had come to Rhode Island, bringing bright sun and a heat that was unusual for mid-October. She wasn't about to complain, though. All too soon her daily run would require a sweat suit, hat, and gloves. Now she delighted in the freedom of shorts and tank top, which allowed her arms and legs to breathe. The sweat that dotted her brow trickled across her temple and down along her hairline. It glistened on her skin, adding glow.

It had been two weeks since she had seen Ross Stephenson, two weeks since his presence had stunned her. He had a way of doing that, she mused, as she dodged a piece of driftwood that had washed up on the beach. The slap of her sneakers on the wet sand evened out.

Eleven years before, Ross had scored a coup, conquering her mind and body within hours. Their encounter two weeks ago had been under vastly different circumstances, but it was nearly as devastating.

The physical attraction between them hadn't diminished. If anything, it was more awesome than before, if her recollection of that kiss in the Wayward Sailor's kitchen was correct. He had to have known how he would affect her, which made his disappearance the next morning all the more unforgiveable.

Chloe hadn't known what to expect—whether Ross would wake her or meet her downstairs for breakfast. She had assumed that, at the very least, he would drive her back to her car. But a maid had awakened her at seven, putting a pot of fresh coffee and a plate of sweet rolls on the small stand by her bed before scurrying back out, and when Chloe reached the front desk, she learned that Ross had already checked out.

She was immediately disappointed, then annoyed with herself. It was better this way. She was too vulnerable, if the previous night's kiss meant anything. Ross made her feel beautiful things, things she didn't deserve. She was alive. That was enough. She reasoned that it was far better that he should be gone from her life.

When the day manager had handed her Ross's note, though, she was livid. "Chloe," he had scrawled in a bold hand, "Had to leave to catch the early plane. Your car is taken care of. Someone from the inn will take you there." It was signed, "Love, Ross." and was punctuated with a period as a statement of fact.

He had no business doing that, had no business using the word love so blithely. But that was the least of it. It seemed that he had paid her tab at the inn and the cost of a new battery and its installation.

She ran on down the beach, struggling to forget about Ross, to push him from mind, to focus on work. But he remained, along with her wounded pride. She had stewed all the way from Rye to Little Compton that morning. On arriving home, she had gotten the address of the Hansen Corporation and sent a check out in the mail that same day, with a note that was much less personal than his.

"Enclosed is a check to cover the expenses I incurred last night and this morning. Chloe Mac-Daniel." She hadn't asked him to take care of her. She didn't need him to take care of her. She didn't want to feel beholden to him in any way, shape, or form, because one thing was clear. She had picked herself up after Crystal's death and built a new life. She wasn't letting anything threaten it.

With firm resolve she made a gentle semicircle and jogged more slowly back toward where she had left her towel on the rocks at the sea side of her home.

As she approached, though, it wasn't the house that caught her eye but the tall figure that moved away from it and began to walk to the beach. She stopped short.

He was dressed in casual navy slacks and a plaid shirt that was unbuttoned at the neck and rolled to the elbows. His dark hair tumbled in disarray across his brow. Even from a distance he looked threatening in a divine kind of way.

He must have been watching for her, must have stood by the living room window until she had come into sight. If Lee hadn't been there to answer the door, he might have left. Now she was caught—and annoyed.

Tipping up a defiant chin, she began walking. Ross made no move to meet her halfway, just watched and waited, but his stance suggested an annoyance of his own, along with a touch of the imperious. Despite his casual clothes, he looked formal.

She came to a halt before him, nodded, and offered a polite "Ross" in greeting, before shifting beyond him to retrieve her towel.

"What in the hell did you do it for, Chloe?" He was annoyed, all right.

"Do what?" She straightened slowly.

His eyes bore into her. "Send that check. You didn't lose a minute, did you? You must have had it in the mail that same afternoon."

"Shouldn't I have?"

"No. There was no need."

"I thought there was. You had no cause to pick up the check, either for the inn or the battery. I'm not helpless. I can take care of myself."

A muscle worked in his jaw. "Then it was a matter of principle?"

"Principle? I wasn't thinking about principle. I simply saw it as my responsibility. It was kind of you to offer to pay, but I feel more comfortable this way. I wanted to take care of it myself."

"Ah. The independent woman. So that's how you intend to live the rest of your life?" he challenged, and drawled, "All by yourself?"

Chloe was startled by the turn of the conversation. "This is crazy," she said. "You show up here, out of the blue, without so much as a civil hello, and start criticizing me? I don't have to defend my lifestyle to you or anyone else!" She turned away, then turned right back, confused. "Why are you here, Ross? Did you come all the way from Park Avenue to call me out for repaying your loan? Little Compton is on the way to nowhere. We're at the tip of a peninsula. So don't tell me you were just passing through."

"No." His features had begun to relax, though his eyes remained clear and direct. "I wanted to see you."

Chloe could deal with the angry Ross more easily than she could with the gentler one. Uncomfortable now, she bent for her towel and straightened holding it tight. "You could have called if you wanted to discuss the Rye Beach Complex. Nothing much will happen until the referendum in November. Unless, of course, you alter your proposal." Satisfied with her minor dig, she began to mop her face and neck.

Ross ignored the barb. "I'm not here on business. I came to see you."

"That's a mistake," she whispered, hearing pain, feeling pain.

He replied as softly. "Then again we differ in opinion." He sighed. "Look, can we walk? Your house seemed pretty crowded. I'd like to talk."

All too aware of a tingling inside, she shook her head, then tore her gaze from his and looked out to sea. "It's not a good idea."

"Just talk?"

"Fine, if it has to do with the complex. Anything else . . ."

"What are you afraid of?" he asked. "I see the same fear in you now that I saw two weeks ago. What is it?"

She shot him a chiding look that said *You're imagining it, I'm not afraid of a thing.*

"Then what can be the harm in talking? What can be so awful about walking along the beach with me for a few minutes?" He tossed his dark head back toward the house. "You have a whole crew in there just waiting to come if you scream."

"I won't scream." She spoke softly, blushed lightly. "It's not my style."

He studied her for what seemed an eternity. "Maybe that's your problem," he finally decided. "You're too composed. Maybe you need a good yell and scream to let it all out."

"Let what all out?"

He took her arm. "Come on. Let's take a walk." He pulled her gently into step beside him, and she went along. After all, what harm could come from a walk on the beach?

One fast glance at Ross supplied an answer. The magnetism was there in all its force, coming from him, tugging at her. If only they had never met before, if only they didn't have a past, there might have been hope.

"What if," he echoed her thoughts with uncanny precision, "we had never met before? Would you feel differently?"

"Maybe." She clutched the ends of the towel that circled her neck. "Would you?" some inner voice made her ask.

"No." There was no hesitancy in his response. "I saw a woman two weeks ago who interested me. I would be here regardless. It's just . . ."

As Chloe waited for his voice to pick up again, their paths crisscrossed her earlier footprints.

Ross easily measured his pace to hers. "It's just what?" she prodded.

He stopped walking. She went a step farther, then turned to face him. He frowned, seeming deliberative. "It's just that after what happened eleven years ago, I feel even more justified . . ."

Her voice rose, as it often did when she was distressed. "Are you saying you feel guilty so long after the fact? Is that why you've come? To ease some long-harbored guilt? Where were you then?" she cried. "Where were you when I—"

She cut herself off. For the very first time she wondered what might have happened had Ross been with her at the time of Crystal's death. It had been late Saturday night, two days after Thanksgiving, when she and Crystal argued, Crystal raced off in her car, the accident happened. By that time Ross was on his way back to Africa. What if he had been with her through the ordeal? Would things have been different?

But he hadn't been with her. There was no changing that fact. She had survived. She had survived. Not Crystal, though.

When she closed her eyes for a moment in search of composure, Ross took her arm and said a quick, "Over there. Those rocks. You should sit down."

"I'm all right—"

"Then I want to sit down! Indulge me!" He led her to a jagged outcropping of rocks. When they were seated on side by side boulders, he said, "Okay. Why don't you tell me about that night— and stop looking at me like I'm crazy. You know what I'm talking about. I know what I experienced that night. I'd like to hear what you did."

"Oh, Ross." She sighed wearily. "I don't want to go into this." She caught the graceful takeoff of a tern from the salt-soaked beach. "It's too beautiful here to rehash the past."

"The past had its moments of beauty, too."

Her head snapped back, but the warmth of his gaze cut off the retort that might have come. Suddenly it seemed pointless to resist his request. It was just a matter of choosing the right words. "The past did have its moments. And, yes, they were beautiful." There was a soft quality in her voice as she returned to that night.

Ross grasped the stone on either side of him. "Had you planned it to happen? When you came toward me from across that room, had you hoped that we'd end up in bed?"

"Beforehand?" She looked up in surprise. "No. I'd never done anything like that before. Oh, we dated plenty and went to our share of parties. But we had never, that is, neither of us had, ah, I mean, I had never . . ."

"I know." He rescued her from her floundering, daring to touch her cheek with the back of his fingers. Instinctively she tipped her face toward his touch, then caught herself and righted her head.

"Were you sorry you did it?" His voice was low, urgent.

"No . . . Yes . . . I don't know," she finally ended in a whisper, tugging at the towel draped about her neck. "I can't give you a simple yes or no. I've never regretted the act itself. It was beautiful."

"Then what is it about me that makes you so uncomfortable?"

The ensuing silence was rich with the sounds of the shore—the lapping of the waves, the cry of the gulls, the rustle of the breeze in the drying leaves of the wild honeysuckle. Each had the potential to soothe, yet Chloe remained tense.

"Seeing you," she finally confessed, "brings back memories of a holiday weekend that was tragic for me."

"Your sister's death."

Her eyes shot to his. "You knew?" And hadn't tried to contact her?

The dark sheen of his hair captured the golden rays of the slow-setting sun. "Yes, I knew, but not until long after I'd returned to Africa. I didn't feel then that it was my place to contact you."

"Why not?" She didn't understand that detachment. He was certainly persistent enough now.

"In the first place," he began, "it was pitiful, how long after the fact I learned of it. Sammy wrote me the news in a letter the following spring." He seemed to hesitate. More quietly, he said, "It was only then that I'd had the guts to ask him about you."

"But why?" she cried.

"Because you weren't the only one to have afterthoughts of that night! From what I could see I had seduced the virgin daughter of my host's best friend. I was twenty-seven. You were eighteen. I should have known better. But the worst of it was that I was glad I hadn't." His voice gentled. "The memory of that night helped me through many a lonely night afterward."

"Oh, Ross," Chloe whispered, feeling a great longing inside. "I wish it hadn't. It's too late to go back."

"I don't want to go back. I want to go ahead. That's why I'm here."

Anguished, she looked down. "It's no good. I can't."

"Can't or won't? We've been through this before. Well," he drew in a breath, "believe this. I may have been immature eleven years ago, running away from something that frightened me, but I won't make the same mistake twice. It was fate that brought us together up at Rye Beach, and I'll be damned if I'm going to let you get away. I've made it my business to find out every possible thing I could about you during the past two weeks. And I know what happened to Crystal."

His words hung in the air. Her eyes begged him to say no more. She bolstered the plea with her low whisper. "Then you can understand why I can't bear to think back on that time."

"It was an accident, Chloe! It wasn't your fault!"

"But she died."

"And you lived, is that it? You can't forgive yourself for that?"

She jumped to her feet. With her heart pounding a thunderous beat, she stared at him for an agonized moment before forcing her feet to move. Her steps were slow at first, then gained speed as the force of habit took over and she jogged toward safer ground.

With pitiful ease, Ross caught up. He caught her elbow, using her own momentum to bring her around. When she faced him at a full stop, he held her by both arms.

"I'm trying to be honest," he said.

"But it hurts. Can't you see that? It hurts!" She was consumed by it, a hurt that was alive and festering. He had to see it anywhere he looked.

"The only way the hurt will stop," he chided gently, "is for you to put the past behind you."

Her eyes filled with tears. "Do you think I haven't tried? Do you think I've spent the past eleven years purposely living with a ghost?"

"Maybe not, but you've done it. You haven't resolved a thing in the eleven years, if that hurt in your eyes is for real. It's your punishment, isn't it? Your punishment for living."

She shook her head and whispered, "No. That's not true!"

"Not true?" he echoed in a voice strangely mellow. "Answer me one thing, Chloe. Have you been with another man since we were together?"

"That's none of your bus—"

"It is so." He took her face in his hands, correctly anticipating her attempt to look away. His touch was gentle but firm. "I was the first. It's my brand that shaped you. How many others were there?"

"That's vulgar!" she cried.

"Maybe. Answer the question."

"I won't. Are you jealous, jealous and guilt-ridden? Well, I don't need either of those traits in the man in my life. I'm doing just fine without—without—" Her limbs trembled.

Ross drew her against him, pressing her cheek to his chest, wrapping his arms around her back. "Without love?" he asked, so softly that she might not have heard him had the word not been on the tip of her tongue.

Incapable of speech for the moment, she simply breathed in the scent that was all male, all Ross. His heart beat steadily by her ear, gradually coaxing her own to slow. His arms enveloped her and lent her strength.

"I tried." She spoke, unsteadily at first. "I dated. I still do." It was easier not having to look at him. "I even tried to go to bed with one of them." She recalled the horror of the moment. "He decided I was frigid."

A deep laugh broke from Ross's throat, a laugh that was strangely hoarse. "That's ridiculous," he crooned into the warmth of her hair, but when he tipped her face up he felt her stiffen. "Oh, no, you don't." His mouth found hers.

She fought him then. Struggling to free herself from the band of his arms, she pushed against his chest, all the while trying to evade his lips, but he was stronger than she was. The more she squirmed, the more he steadied her. His lips stroked hers, demanding the kind of response that he alone knew she had in her.

When her physical strength waned, Chloe tried passivity. The last thing she wanted was a repeat of the night in New Hampshire or, worse, that fateful night back in New Orleans. She had no right, she told herself, no right!

"Come on, Chloe," Ross growled against her lips. "Ease up."

"Don't—"

She shouldn't have said anything. The tiny parting of her lips gave him the opening he needed, and then she didn't have a chance. His tongue invaded her mouth, spreading its sweetness deep. She told herself that it was physical, that she could resist if she wanted to enough, but her body betrayed her. It swayed toward him, weak with wanting.

From an odd defense mechanism, her mind went blank. It was as though the battle between guilt and desire created a mental void. In that void there was nothing but Ross and his body, the lips that caressed her, arms that held her gently, legs that supported her. Out of that void came her response, slowly, surely, and Ross had won. Her lips moved against his, tasting, savoring. The corners of his mouth, his firm lips, his tongue—one small nibble led to another until she returned his kiss with matching passion.

"Oh, Ross," she breathed raggedly when his lips left hers to trail fire along the sensitive cord of her neck.

"That's it, princess."

"No." That word. That past.

His breath warmed her ear. "You'll always be my princess, Chloe." He nibbled at her lobe. "It has nothing to do with the past. Right now you're my princess." With a groan, he pressed her to him. She felt his desire as she tried to deny her own, but that same coil of need gnawed within her. She was on the verge of losing control.

"No!" Her scream echoed back through her with such force that only Ross's arms kept her standing. As she sagged against him, he eased down onto the sand, turning her to sit with her back to his chest, her knees bent and bounded by his. He said nothing, just held her, his arms wrapped around her middle.

Chloe couldn't have moved if she'd tried. Drained by emotional strain, she closed her eyes and breathed in deeply of the slow-cooling air.

When Ross spoke long moments later, she was surprised to hear humor in his voice. "Not bad for a novice."

"What?"

"That scream. For someone who says she doesn't do that kind of thing, you sure let loose!"

She let out a breath and grinned, feeling oddly calm. "I guess I did. You have a way of doing the weirdest things to me."

"I certainly hope so," he drawled.

"Ross—"

"Shh. I've heard enough from you for a while. I want you to listen."

"But—"

"Shh! I have something to say."

"You—umph!" The breath was forced from her by a squeeze to her middle. She didn't try to speak again.

"Better," he said. "Now, listen. I realize that you

need time, and I'll give you that. But I'm not leaving. Not this time. I want to get to know you, and I want you to get to know me. We blew it on that score last time. But yesterday was one thing, today's another, and they're different, Chloe, they're different."

She liked the sound of that. Didn't know if she believed it. But it was fine for the moment. Same thing with sitting against one another this way, looking out over the last of the sunset's flaming rays. Ross provided support. And heat. She was acutely aware of his long legs, his strong arms, his broad chest, his warm breath. She might not have a right to do it, but she savored the peace of the moment.

So maybe today was different. Certainly they were eleven years older, maybe even worlds wiser. But Crystal had been an intrinsic part of her life. To forget her would be wrong. It was more a matter of acceptance. Could she accept the past and learn to live with it?

"Well?" Ross's baritone hummed by her ear.

"Well, what?" She had reached her saturation point and couldn't agonize anymore.

He nudged her ribs. "Don't you have anything to say for yourself?"

Her long pause was nearly as effective as the sigh that followed it. "I can speak now?"

"Speak."

"That's a beautiful sunset," she mused aloud. "It's a treat at this time of year, all warm and golden. Do you have any idea what would happen if the ozone layer were to be destroyed by the haphazard release of freon gas?"

4

"Chlo . . . eee."

Before Ross could respond, a call of concern came from far down the beach.

"It's Lee," Chloe explained as her partner loped toward where she and Ross sat. Ross made no move to hold her back when she slid from his grip and jumped to her feet.

The timing couldn't have been better. With those legs framing hers and the strength of that body a serious temptation, her diversion into environmental quandaries would have been temporary at best. Lee's appearance was a godsend.

Aware that Ross had risen beside her, Chloe kept her eyes on the approaching figure. "You met Lee at the house, didn't you?" she asked.

"No," he said with something of a grunt. "Another character let me in and directed me to you. Is this some kind of commune you live in?"

Lee's booming call spared Chloe from having to answer. "Is everything all right, Chloe?" He covered the last of the distance at a more cautious walk, making no effort to disguise his wariness of an equally wary Ross. "It's getting dark. I was beginning to worry."

Chloe absently clutched her left wrist, a habit dating back to the days when she wore a watch. Her fingers easily circled the bone. "Oh, my. I'm sorry. I lost track of the time. We were going to—" Suddenly aware that the two men were staring at each other, she interrupted the thought and said, "Lee, this is Ross Stephenson. We knew each other a long time ago. Ross heads the corporation responsible for the Rye Beach proposal." She looked at Ross. "This is Lee Haight. Lee and I co-own ESE."

For a brief instant, she pictured the two men squaring off, and there was that moment's antagonism. She was relieved when Ross extended his hand. It was met by an equally large one of Lee's.

Chloe was struck by those hands, but they were only the start. The physical similarities between the two men, each of whom had been instrumental in shaping her life, was amazing. Both were tall and lean; both had athletic builds. While Ross's dark hair had faint wisps of gray at the sideburns, Lee's highlights were more auburn, but both men were tanned and inordinately good-looking. Only their dress differentiated their approaches to life. Whereas Ross was the image of the casual male of the more traditional school, Lee was, in appearance, reminiscent of that earlier, more nonconformist phase through which the other had passed. While Ross wore slacks, Lee wore denim. While Ross wore a sports shirt, Lee wore a T-shirt emblazoned with an apt EARTHMAN. Ross wore well-kept loafers, Lee had on a pair of battered running shoes. And then there was that neatly trimmed beard of Lee's that stretched from ear to ear, much as Ross's had on the night Chloe had met him.

It had never occurred to her to compare the two men before, but on all counts the likeness was astounding.

Apparently Ross saw it, too. He grinned slowly, almost slyly. "It looks like Chloe's taste in men hasn't changed all that much, after all," he said, with such a lack of malice that Lee relaxed a little.

"I intend to take that statement at its most positive, friend. This little lady is very near and dear to me." He threw a protective arm about Chloe's shoulder, drawing her to him with his customary possessiveness. She had always liked that, and did even more so now. His presence made her feel less vulnerable. She chuckled when Lee added, "Are you friend or foe?"

"Friend, by all means," Ross replied.

"Then I take it you're not here on business," Lee concluded. "And you can't be passing through."

Chloe laughed this time. "I've been through all

that with him, Lee. He knows precisely where he is."

Lee glanced her way. "Sounds ominous." He looked at Ross. "How long are you in for?"

"I was hoping to spend the weekend here," Ross answered with a calm that had the opposite effect on Chloe. Her stomach was suddenly filled with butterflies. They fluttered wildly when those amber eyes turned to her. "If Chloe is free."

Chloe didn't know whether Lee sensed her internal turmoil, but she was eternally grateful for the arm that tightened around her shoulders. "You'll have a fight on your hands," he said. "I have a prior claim on her. Your big corporation may be able to do without you for the weekend, but our small one isn't so generous." Looking down at her, he said, "There were several calls for you. Alabama called again on that toxic waste burning problem. I told them you'd have an answer for them by Monday."

Chloe nodded, sighing her uncertainty on the Alabama matter. "And the other calls?"

"Derry Township called on the lecture series at the community college. They want to know when the printed material will be ready to be copied. Jay called from Pittsburgh to say that he should be back on Sunday, and Debbie will have the statistics on the sinkhole study for you to see tomorrow."

"Whoa. She sure got that together fast." She told Ross, "Debbie is the newest member of the firm. She just got her degree. Her working knowledge of computers is much better than Lee's or mine." She frowned. "Boy, would I like to take more courses."

"Why don't you?" Ross asked.

"No time. Lee and I have worked our butts off trying to make ESE a functioning enterprise." She shot a look at her partner. "I think we're finally seeing the light at the end of the tunnel."

His grimace took her by surprise. Instead of agreement, she saw sudden doubt. "That's another point of discussion for the weekend," Lee informed her softly, squeezing her arm a final time before releasing her. "But, hey, it's getting dark. Let's carry on inside. Want to stay for dinner, Ross?"

Chloe bent to retie a shoelace that needed no retying. She didn't want Ross staying for dinner. She wanted to return to her life, and that meant having him leave and stay gone. Naturally, he had other ideas.

"That would be fine," he said with gratitude.

But Chloe sensed something in him. As the three of them walked back down the beach to her house, she saw the tension on Ross's face. His eyes met hers, and she was again grateful for Lee's presence.

Then Lee turned traitorous. With a grin, he said, "There's some great wine in the cellar, Chloe. The steaks are already on the counter. Why don't you take another one from the freezer? I'll meet you in the kitchen." And he loped off.

Before she could follow, Ross wrapped a hand around her long ponytail and held her in place.

"What was that all about?" he asked with a scowl. "You told me you lived alone."

She stared straight ahead, looking after Lee. "I do."

Ross moved closer. His head lowered to hers. "Then why is that fellow so damned at home in your house? He sounds like he's the live-in chef—between the wine and the steaks. What other services does he perform?"

She didn't like his implication. Still staring at the house, she said, "He's good enough to bring the trash to the dump once a week and put on the storm windows when winter comes and pump out the basement when it floods. In addition to which, his office is located here, as is mine, and the rest of ESE." Risking pain in her scalp, she turned her head and looked at him. "I thought you learned something about me this week. It's a simple fact that the address of ESE and my home address are the same."

He had released her hair. "I know that. I didn't bother to look up the home address of your partner, though. For all I knew he lived here with you."

"I told you I lived alone." With an impatience unusual to her, Chloe stalked onward toward the house. Ross was quickly beside her.

"So where does he live?"

"Over there." She pointed to a small house that was farther back from the beach but no more than several hundred yards from Chloe's.

"Convenient," Ross mused dryly.

Of her own accord this time, she stopped in her tracks. "It happens to be very convenient." She glared at his all-too-handsome face, which, to her chagrin, seemed suddenly amused. "He's a good friend, an able geologist, and a very trusting soul." When Ross dared to smile, she cried, "What's so funny?"

"Not funny." He laughed nonetheless. "Refreshing. The way you've repressed so many other things, it's nice to know you can be so outspoken. But then, you were quite good up there at Rye Beach."

"Quite good?" she asked smugly. "You'd better start rethinking those plans of yours or those good folks up there are going to vote down your entire project. It doesn't have as much to do with my being good as with the truth of my points."

"That was one of the things I had wanted to discuss this weekend," he said. He began walking toward the house again, bringing her along with a feather touch at the back of her waist.

She eyed him skeptically. "I thought this was a strictly personal visit."

"It is. This is a personal business matter."

"A personal business matter?" She shot a glance skyward. "Lord help me. What next?" The faint pressure of his hand on her back was ample suggestion. "Forget I asked that. A personal business matter. Okay. We can discuss it during dinner."

"I was hoping to discuss it privately. I actually was hoping to take you out to dinner."

"You should have called first."

"Would you have accepted if I had?"

"No. Lee and I have a standing dinner meeting every Friday night to review the week's happenings."

They had reached the base of the fieldstone steps that led to Chloe's back porch. Ross paused on the first step. "And those others I saw here this afternoon. Who were they?"

"Workers on our various projects."

"Partners in the firm?"

She shook her head. "We hire part-time people. They're mostly students, master's candidates from local schools like URI and Brown."

The pale blue of dusk was quickly giving way to the darker purples of evening in a star-filled sky. Only the spill of pale gold light from the kitchen window lit Ross's features now. It left his lines more clear-cut, his profile more distinct and dramatic. Chloe was intrigued.

"I admire you for your dedication," he said.

She continued to study him. "Do I hear wistfulness?"

His chuckle was suspiciously poignant. "Maybe. There are times—ach, that's a whole other thing."

When she would have pursued it, Lee's shout jarred her. "Chloe!" Her head whipped around. "Where are the matches? The pilot light is out on the broiler. I can't get it lit."

Ross leaned close and murmured, "And here I thought he was the one who always came to your rescue."

She turned to defend Lee, only to find Ross's lips a breath from hers. His eyes were glowing, his body warm though the heat of the day was gone, and her mouth was suddenly dry. "I think I'd better give him a hand. Pray we're not out of matches."

Her response was meant as humor, because she wasn't telling Ross the truth. Oh, yes, Lee was a willing handyman, able in nine cases out of ten. But they had a running gag over that tenth. Chloe was convinced, and had told Lee as much, that his occasional flub was intentional, his way of reminding her that he needed her, too. He never denied it. And Chloe always indulged him. Emotionally, he gave her so much. She liked giving a little some of that back.

Without further pause, she ran up the steps. It was only when she reached the top and started for the door that Ross caught her hand. He pressed something into it. She looked down at a book of matches.

"You smoke?"

"Actually," he said with a wry twist of his lips, "I carry matches around with me just in case a pilot light goes out."

"Do you smoke?"

"Through my eyes, when I'm angry."

"Ross, do you?"

"Smoke? No."

She sighed. "That's good. This is a nonsmoking house. If you wanted to smoke you'd have to sneak one in the john, or stay out here with the chipmunks."

"That's some choice. Good thing I don't have to make it. As it happens," he informed her, "my only vice is sex. Do we have to sneak that in the john, too?"

She might have choked if she'd been eating. But she recovered quickly, shook her head, and muttered a soft "Incorrigible ..." as she pulled the screen open. She took refuge in the kitchen, where her loyal protector, Lee, was waiting.

And he filled that role repeatedly throughout the evening, taking over for her when she was distracted. He was an able conversationalist, a gracious host. She trembled to think what would have happened had she and Ross been alone in the house. She was too vulnerable, too susceptible where Ross was concerned. If she hadn't known it before, she learned it that evening.

It started before dinner, when she left the two men and went off to shower. She put on a pair of jeans and a western-style blouse that had breast pockets and a decoratively stitched yoke. Her intent was to be cool and at ease. The finished product, though, spoke of homespun femininity. Had it been the pale pink of the blouse, she later asked herself? Or the way the seasoned denims outlined her hips? Whatever, she caught Ross's attention. Her first step into the living room, where the men were nursing drinks while the steaks grilled, brought Ross's eyes her way for a perusal that set her pulse hammering. Where Chloe's peace of mind was concerned, it was downhill from there. She wanted to tune him out, but she couldn't.

The talk centered on business matters. Sitting quietly in a peacock chair, Chloe learned that Ross's headquarters were indeed in New York, but that there were corporate branches in the South and in the West.

She tried to imagine it. "You must live out of a suitcase a good deal of your time."

"I'm used to it. Don't forget, when I was a kid my family was shuttled around by the Army." At

Lee's prodding, Ross elaborated on his background. Chloe found herself wondering if he had ever settled down, even for a short time, or if he ever would. She found herself wondering how as compelling and attractive a man had avoided the lure of a wife, a home, a family. When she was caught in the act of admiring him, Ross smiled in what she swore was a knowing way.

And so went the evening. Lee talked with Ross, and Ross talked with Lee. Chloe listened, joining in from time to time, trying to fight admiration without much success.

Why Ross? she asked herself at one point. Why not Lee? The two were as physically alike as brothers. But then, why had Ross been attracted to Chloe rather than Crystal? Or had he? Had Crystal been right? Had it been a case of his taking what was offered by whichever sister came forward?

That question nagged. *Had* her being with Ross been pure chance? A simple turn of fate? But what about that coin? There was nothing coincidental about Chloe winning the toss. And Ross—had he been looking at Chloe rather than at her identical twin sister? Had it all been by design, or had it been by pure chance?

She was distracted as the evening waned, unaware of looks of concern sent her way. When Lee said, "I'm takin' off now, Chloe," she was startled. Her head came up. Unsure, she straightened.

"I'm sorry," she apologized softly. "I'm afraid I haven't been much help. We haven't even gone over those things we should have."

"No problem." He smiled. "We'll do it tomorrow." Taking his cue from the disquieted look in her eyes, he turned to Ross. "Are you staying here tonight?"

"Yes."

"No."

They spoke at the same time. Chloe hurried on. "No, Ross. You can't stay here." She was determined. "There's one bedroom and one bed, and I need it."

"Why don't you stay with me, friend?" Lee offered—and for the second time that evening, Chloe could have disowned him. She wanted Ross to leave. Out of sight was out of mind. Lee's offer only complicated things.

Naturally, Ross accepted the invitation. "No imposition?"

"No imposition. The sofa in the living room opens into a bed. The back door will be open. Chloe will point you in the right direction." Before she could protest, Lee reached the door. "Good night, folks." He grinned, letting himself out with a flourish.

With a steadying breath, Chloe settled deeper into her high-backed chair, tucked her feet under her, forced her fingers to relax against the broad wicker arms, and looked across the room at Ross.

He spoke softly. "You really do look like a princess in that chair. Those peacock markings could as easily be a crown of gold as a swirl of wicker. Are you comfortable?" His eyes were gleaming, mocking.

"No," she answered honestly. "You know I'm not."

His grin held no apology. "That's a shame. I don't want you to be miserable through the entire weekend."

"You can't stay all weekend!"

"Why not? I have a place to sleep. That Lee's a good guy."

"Too good!" she grumbled. "I thought I could trust him."

Ross sat forward, elbows on his thighs, fingers steepled. "That's what puzzles me. I'm sure you can trust him, but I can't figure out for the life of me why."

Chloe instantly came to Lee's defense. "He's been a true friend to me."

"Why only a true friend? Why not a lover?"

"Lee doesn't want that from a woman."

"You mean, he prefers—"

"No. No, Ross. Don't twist things." Beneath his stare, her own insides twisted. "Lee was married once. He has two children. He and his wife divorced five years ago. She lives in St. Louis."

"Ah. Once burned . . . okay, I'll accept that."

"How kind," she murmured, but she was annoyed enough to see an opening and take it. "What about you? In the eleven years since I knew you when, what have you done along similar lines? Should I assume you've developed odd preferences?"

The instant she said it, she knew it was a mistake. Good humor faded fast from Ross's face. When he stood and approached her, she struggled to avoid cringing into the chair. There was a hard look to him.

"Would that make you trust me more?" he murmured. He towered above her for a minute, then bent over. His hands covered hers on the arms of the chair. His face was too near. "Sorry to disappoint you, but my preferences are still for the opposite sex." His lips moved closer. Chloe looked down to escape them, but his long body filled her view. Everywhere she moved her eyes, she saw him, one point more alarming than the next. If it wasn't the vee of his chest, with its wisps of dark hair edging alongside the tab of his collar, it was the breadth of his shoulders or the lean tapering of his middle or the casual set of his hips. Those hips told their own story. She tore her gaze away, completely convinced of his preference.

He grinned. "Any further questions?"

The slight shake of her head was enough to bring his lips into contact with her cheek, and

Chloe was suddenly conflicted. Pull away. Move closer. Keep your eyes shut. Look at him. Look at him. Look at him.

She looked. His eyes held gentleness now. And the same desire she felt. So close. So far away. Kiss me. Don't.

He did. Very, very lightly. A ghost of a touch with shuddering intensity. Chloe's eyes were shut, her lips parted. To taste him once more . . .

When he kissed her again, his tenderness incited her need. She moved closer, clung to him with her own lips, drank in the tang of his mouth, so moist and strong yet soft. His tongue touched hers briefly before he raised his head.

"Definitely my preference." He spoke thickly, his breathing uneven.

Chloe was momentarily disoriented. It was a minute before reality returned. Then she was appalled. "What am I doing?" she asked, not realizing she'd spoken aloud. "What am I doing?"

"Letting yourself live," came the husky but gentle declaration.

Burying her face in her hands, she struggled to understand what had just happened. She couldn't face him, much less herself. Easier to hide behind the cascade of hair that fell forward, shielding her from the world.

Lost in silent self-reproach Chloe was unaware that he had moved away and returned to the sofa.

He was waiting, listening, when she finally raised her head.

"Why are you doing this to me?" she pleaded softly. "Why can't you just leave me alone?"

He frowned. "Funny, I've asked myself the same question a dozen times in the last two weeks." He studied his knuckles, seeming to struggle. "It's like for the first time in years, I care."

"What do you mean?" she asked falteringly.

"You asked me what I've done with myself during the past years." He gave a snort of disgust. "I haven't been quite as noble as you. There have been women over the years."

She had assumed that, and felt no resentment. There was a certain solace in the knowledge that when all was said and done, he was still attracted to her. After all, he was magnificent. More than one of those women must have tried to tie him down.

"Didn't you find anyone special?" she asked quietly.

Ross was just as quiet. "Some I liked more than others. But, no, there was no one special. No one who meant enough to tempt me to change my lifestyle. I'm on the road all the time. I do own an old brownstone in Manhattan, but I doubt if I spend a total of three months a year there. Hotel rooms, friends' apartments, rented suites—that's been home for the past few years."

"It served your purpose."

"Yes." The amber eyes that held hers pierced her heart. They said much more, all of it silent, all of it mind bending. In the insanity of a fleeting instant, she wanted . . . she wanted . . . What did she want?

Ross sighed. "I am a successful businessman." It was a statement of fact, devoid of arrogance. "But that's not enough."

She followed his thoughts. "I can't help you, Ross."

"Can't?"

"Won't. If you're looking for a wife and a family, a home in the country, maybe a few dogs and horses, even sheep, you'll have to look elsewhere. I can't be anything but this."

His gaze sharpened. "Did I mention those things? Or are they what you wanted once? Haven't you ever wished for a husband who loves you, children, pets, friends, property? What do you want from life?"

"What I have right now. I don't want to look back, and I won't look ahead. I like this life. I'm content."

"Are you?" he challenged. "Don't you ever stop to wonder what it might have been like—"

"No," Chloe said with force and pushed herself out of the chair. "I didn't ask you to come here, Ross. I didn't ask you to stay. As of right now"—she pointed at the floor for emphasis—"I don't care what you do, but don't expect to change the way I see the world and my life. I've done just fine on my own for the past eleven years. I plan to do it a while longer." Her hand was shaking. She jammed it into the back pocket of her jeans. "I'm going to bed. Let yourself out." With a whirl that sent her hair flaring out behind, she strode from the room, ran up the stairs to her room, and firmly closed the door.

Trembling uncontrollably, she collapsed onto the bed and stared at the ceiling. Her ragged breathing was the only sound that broke the night's quiet—that, and the opening and closing of the front door when Ross left the house.

For what seemed like hours she agonized, locked in silent battle with a horde of private ghosts. If only she had never seen Ross again. To be free, once more, of this gnawing at mind and body.

But she had seen him again and, if he stuck to his plan, would see more of him before he left. There was only one solution, as she saw it. Indifference. What man would put up with that for long? Indifference. It would turn him off, wouldn't it? Surely then he would leave her in peace.

She awoke the next morning on an optimistic note, showered, dressed, and sailed downstairs for breakfast. It was with momentary dismay that she found her kitchen in use—until she recalled the night's resolve, tilted up her chin, and advanced.

5

"Ah," she said as she helped herself to a cup of the coffee he had brewed, "you've made yourself at home."

His grin was as bright as the morning sun that slanted across the porch beyond the screen. "It's a luxury. I'm enjoying it. It's not every day that I get to putter around a cozy kitchen, much less wait on a princess."

"Flattery will get you nowhere." She hoped, prayed it was so. By way of diversion, she eyed the stove. "Bacon, eggs, home fries? You're going to eat all that?"

"With your help."

"Ohhhh, no. After a breakfast like that I'd barely be able to keep my eyes open. I have too many things to do—"

"—for which you need energy. And, anyway," he called over his shoulder as he turned the bacon, "if you don't eat breakfasts like this, why such a full stock of goodies? Lee's refrigerator was bare."

"So that's it, huh?" she asked, eyes narrowing. "You're starved and my old buddy Lee couldn't help you out?" She chuckled. "Lee eats out. A lot."

"Here?"

"Do you see him here now?" she shot back.

"I haven't seen him today, period. He's not upstairs, is he?"

Shaking her head, she turned toward the large bay window, whose broad seat was her favorite perch. "That doesn't deserve an answer." Sipping her coffee, she spoke absently. "As for the state of my ice box, I eat in. A lot. Eggs make terrific dinner omelets, bacon a great BLT, and potatoes are most definitely to be baked, then scooped, mashed with a little Parmesan cheese and cream, restuffed, dotted with butter, and broiled until delicately browned on top."

The silence that followed her recitation was enough to get her to look back. Ross's expression was one of amused astonishment. "You must have memorized the cookbook."

"No. I just happen to like my potatoes that way, and I do it a lot."

Ross leaned back against the counter, arms folded across his chest. "Would you make them like that for me some time—maybe with a few lamb chops, some fresh broccoli, a little wine?"

He looked dangerous, newly showered and wearing jeans and a black turtleneck sweater. But

Chloe had taken a vow of indifference. He's just a friend, she told herself, no different from Lee. Calmly enough, she said, "I make a meal of the potatoes. If you'd like to do up the rest, be my guest." She settled on the window seat and looked out at the beach. "It's another beautiful day."

"Uh-huh." His voice was muffled. He had turned back to his cooking. Too soon he was addressing her again. "Sleep well?"

"Not bad." Once she had fallen asleep. "How about you?"

He had turned to reach for plates from the cupboard. "About the same."

It was an odd choice of words, she mused, unless she was so transparent that he could see her thoughts. If there was smugness on his face, though, she couldn't see it. He was cooking. All she saw was his back. There was a full head of thick and vibrant dark hair, a torso whose firmness was shown off by the snug fit of his sweater, a pair of lean denim hips and long, sturdy legs, not to mention well-worn leather boots.

She took a deep, steadying breath. If he had dressed to kill on purpose, she could resist. She wasn't buying what he had to offer. She wasn't.

"All set?" Grinning, he placed two brimming plates on the table. When she gaped at hers in dismay, he added a gentle, "Don't worry. Whatever you can't finish, I will."

She pushed away from the window seat with a grimace. "You'd better get started then. I'm nearly finished." She held up her drained coffee cup. "This is all I usually have, with a slice of toast or a muffin." Still, she took a seat opposite him. She stared at the plate, decided that the eggs looked pretty good, and took a bite.

"Do the people you work with know about your past?"

Her eyes flew to his, warning, then haunted. She gave him a wan smile. "You make it sound lurid." She pushed home fries around her plate. "They know where I come from—some even know that I had a sister. Lee knows most of the story. But the lovely thing about my life here is that the people I know see me for what I am today. It's easier not having to constantly contend with the past."

Ross seemed puzzled. "Why do you assume you'd have to do that anywhere? It's been eleven years, Chloe. The world goes on. People accept change. You seem to be the only one who can't move on."

Chloe set down her fork. She took an angry breath. "I look in the mirror every morning. How can I forget? How can my family forget? How can those people we knew as kids forget, when they see Crystal in my face?" When sitting still took more strength than she had, she rose. "And why should I forget? Crystal was my sister. More than that . . ." She fell silent. Turning her back on Ross, she walked slowly to the window. The sight of the surf rolling onto the beach was calming.

"I'm really not like this," she murmured, speaking to herself and, yes, to him. "Morbidity isn't my style. I loved Crystal. She was my twin. Few people can understand what it meant to me to lose her."

"Maybe that's because you don't share your feelings very often." His voice was suddenly close behind her. The warmth of his body reached out. When he slid his arms around her waist and drew her back against him, she felt sheltered.

"I don't know exactly why I'm doing it now," she whispered. "Maybe it's because you've come out of that past to haunt me." She turned in his arms. Tipping her head up, she studied one strong feature after another. "Is that what you've done—come to haunt me?"

"No, Chloe." He smiled briefly, sadly. The rest of him was exquisitely tender. "I told you yesterday. I want to go forward, not back. I'm beginning to wonder about you, though. You may have to go back, to resolve all those things in your mind, before you can move on."

"But I've done so well up until now," she protested. Without thinking twice, she had put her hands on his chest. They were content to absorb his strength.

"You have. Maybe this was inevitable, though. Whether it was me or something else, you'd have had to face it sooner or later."

"It's not that bad."

"No?"

There was no censure in his tone, no pity in his gaze. He touched her cheek for a fleeting instant, then stepped away. With an exaggerated sigh, he looked at their forgotten breakfast.

"I'd better get this cleaned up. You have to get to work."

Chloe watched him move from table to sink, table to sink, and all she could think was that he'd had the opportunity, but he hadn't kissed her. He had done something else that felt oddly the same. But he hadn't kissed her. She was marveling at that as she headed for the door, bound for her office.

"Chloe?" She looked back. Ross was approaching with her mug in his hand. "Here's a refill. Take it with you?"

She did, and it helped—both the warming brew and the thoughtfulness behind it. And then, once she was settled in her office, she was safe, firmly rooted in the present. There were reports to read, studies to review, proposals to consider. The more she worked, the better she felt. For the first time since having done the lab work earlier that week, she studied the sediment analysis of samples taken along an increasingly unstable portion of the Cape Cod National Seashore.

"Problems?" This from Debbie Walker, who popped her head in shortly after eleven.

"Hi, Deb, Come on in." She smiled at her petite, sandy-haired associate. "It's the Cape analysis. I was just studying the results of the work I did last week. I have the grain sizes of the sand pretty much divided by sections. Boy, they really botched it."

" 'They' being the people who put that parking lot so close to the cliff?"

Chloe sighed. "It's begun to erode already, and the locals want to sue. According to my calculations, they have a case."

"Will you be called in to testify?"

"I'm not sure. I have to work this report up into some kind of written form. Depending on what happens when they read it, whether or not the matter can be settled first, it may not make it to court." She sat back. "It's a shame that we seem to learn things after the fact. If only those developers had gotten a geologist to advise them at the start."

Debbie smiled. "You make a good crusader. I wish I could present my case as well as you do."

"I wish I could handle those computers as well as you do," Chloe returned. "Come on. Let's take a look at your statistics."

They spent the next half hour reviewing the

work Debbie had done. Between them, they came up with a plan of attack on both the sinkhole in question and the people in a position to do something about it. Suitably buoyed, and with her work cut out for her, Debbie left. She was replaced moments later by a slightly groggy-looking Josh Anderson.

Chloe grinned. "Late night last night?"

"Don't you know it," Josh murmured. "But I have to discuss this curriculum guide with you. If the preliminaries are all right, I'd like to work out more of the details."

Chloe's arched brow spoke volumes, as did the slow perusal she gave the casually disheveled graduate student. "You're up to it?" With great effort she stifled a broader grin. Josh was a favorite of hers. Several years her junior, he was working toward his degree at Brown. This was his second year working part-time at ESE.

His proposed high-school geology curriculum was as fine as any she could have hoped ESE would produce.

Now he lowered his voice. "I'd really be up to it if I could take a swig of the coffee that smells so good in the kitchen."

"Why don't you?"

He kept his voice low. "There's a watchdog out there."

"In the kitchen?"

"In the living room. Tall guy, dark hair, dark eyes. He doesn't look happy with the traffic in here. Who is he? And what's he doing in our house?"

For the better part of the morning Chloe had pushed Ross from mind. Now, revived by the work that she loved, she was able to chuckle at Josh's reference.

"He's a friend," she answered simply.

"You're sure about that?"

"I'm sure. Go on out and get your coffee. If he starts to snarl, you can send him in here."

Josh's face took on a dubious I-hope-you-know-what-you're-doing look. Nonetheless, he drew up to his full sixty-seven inches, squared his shoulders, and made as grand an exit as was possible for someone going to face the proverbial giant. With a helpless grin, Chloe sat back in her chair, elbows on its arms, fingers comfortably laced.

So Ross had decided to spend the morning in her living room. She wondered if he was bored, maybe annoyed that she was carrying on as usual, perhaps growing impatient. Her grin turned smug.

"You wanted to see me?" His deep voice rumbled in from the door.

Her grin remained. "Who, me?"

He searched the room. "I don't see anyone else in here, for a change. They may not technically live here, but they run in and out all day, don't they?"

"It's an open office, you might say."

"I do say. Say, when will you be done?"

"Done?" she echoed innocently, then gestured toward the desktop. "Lord knows. I have two reports to look through yet. And Josh will be back. Here he is." His timing was perfect. "Josh, meet Ross." As the two shook hands, Chloe stared at the appalling discrepancy in their heights. No wonder Josh had been intimidated; not only did Ross tower over him, but their respective physiques were about as alike as night and day.

Instinctively protective of Josh, she pointed him to a chair. Then she said, "Ross, would you excuse us? We'll be a little while."

"I'll be waiting." He smiled as though he had caught onto the game and was playing. Then he turned and left.

Josh wasn't thick. "Listen, Chloe, are you sure you wouldn't rather go over this another time?"

"What?" she ribbed him gently. "And waste the effort it took for you to pull yourself out of bed? Carry on!"

It was a full hour later when Josh finally left. Chloe walked him to the door and had only enough time to note that Ross was occupied with a briefcase of his own, before Lee bounded through the living room. He delivered a wave in passing to Ross, looped an arm about Chloe's waist, and corralled her back into her office.

"It's about time you're free," he scolded good-naturedly. "You're a busy lady."

Chloe smiled. "I'm all yours now. I want to show you—"

The look on his face cut her off. "There's something we have to discuss first. I think," he said, giving care to each word, "that we have a problem."

"A problem?" She frowned. "What problem?"

Eying her warily, he said, "I had two cancellations yesterday."

"Cancellations?"

"That's right. The schools. They don't have the money to finance us for the next semester."

She sat straighter. "Are you serious?"

"Very."

"But I thought—"

"So did I."

"I just sent Josh out of here with a great proposal. You mean to say that he won't be able to apply it?"

"Not in Hingham or Westerly he won't. There are still the wealthier communities . . ." His voice trailed off, his implication clear.

"But not for long. That's it, isn't it? You think we're headed down a dead-end street?"

"Unless the powers that dole out money for education loosen up. They're thinking A, B, Cs.

We're talking H, I, Js. We're strictly elective, they say. A luxury they can't afford."

Chloe's mind raced ahead. "A good third of our work is through the public schools. Oh, boy. We'd better rethink that."

"Smart girl."

"Private enterprise," she announced without hesitation.

"Come again? Business isn't our field."

Chloe laughed at the confusion on Lee's bearded face. "No. But I said it to Debbie earlier this morning and I meant it. What we need is to affiliate ourselves with corporations as resident geologists, be the geologists-on-call for several of these large development corporations. You know, like—"

"—the Hansen Corporation?"

The thought took her off-guard. "No," she said with deliberate care. "I was thinking more of firms like Cabot and Walker, or Fennimen East."

But Lee was grinning. "What's wrong with the Hansen Corporation?"

"Nothing," she said, but rethought her answer when Lee was clearly disbelieving. She lowered her voice. "What's wrong with the Hansen Corporation is that Ross Stephenson is its president."

"So?"

"Lee," she pleaded, "Ross is a friend. I would no more ask him to hire ESE than . . . than . . ." She went silent, at a loss for words. She was hoping to survive a single weekend with Ross. She couldn't begin to imagine working with him on an ongoing basis.

Lee grew serious. "What is he to you, Chloe?"

She sighed, giving up the struggle to find excuses. "We knew each other before Crystal died."

"He's the one, isn't he?" There was only kindness in Lee's voice, yet his words jolted her.

"What?" she whispered.

"He's the one—the man in your life."

"There is no man in my life. You know that."

Lee grew gentler. "Over the years, I've learned a lot about you. You've told me about your sister, that she died, that you rarely visit your family back in New Orleans. But you never talk about men. You're a beautiful person, Chloe. I know it, and he knows it." He tilted his head toward the living room. "I dare you to look me in the eye and deny that there was ever anything between the two of you."

She couldn't lie. Not to Lee. "I can't do that. But, whatever it was, it's over."

"You think so?"

"Yes." She said it firmly, and held her head the same way.

Lee studied her for a long minute, before making a show of wiping his hands together. "Well, then, I guess that settles that." He graciously redirected the conversation to safer ground. "I do agree with you that the private business sector could be a promising outlet. I'll be in Washington next week to work with the Coast Guard on the Gulf project. Let me see what nosing around I can do while I'm there."

"How much longer will the training project take?"

"With the government, that's a good question. And when it comes to oil spill cleanups, no amount of training is ever enough. I would guess the present phase will take another few months at least."

Chloe contemplated those coming few months. Unthinkingly, she glanced toward the door.

Lee headed that way. "I can take the hint, pretty lady." His hand was on the knob before she could call him back. "Anything else can wait. Have fun!" He left with a wink.

"Lee! Wait—"

But one dark head was replaced by another. "At last," Ross said and closed the office door. "Alone at last."

Chloe forced herself to sit back slowly. "I hadn't realized you would hang around all morning. I hope you weren't bored."

"Actually"—he circled her desk to plant himself on the corner nearest her—"I went over some papers of my own. I'm a good loser, for a morning." He cocked his head toward the door. "Ready to go?"

"Go? Where?"

"Oh"—he looked out the window in amusement—"I thought you could show me around town. I'm a stranger to these parts."

Judging from the confidence he exuded, it was a wonder that any parts were strange to him. Chloe couldn't ignore the thread of excitement that he had brought with him into the room. Indifference, she reminded herself. But it was a tough order.

Standing quickly, she tried to remedy the situation. "I wish I could help, but I still have—" A strong arm caught her waist. Before she could say another word, she was imprisoned between his thighs.

"All work and no play—"

"Makes a successful scientist."

"And a very dull woman."

She frowned, unwittingly taking his bait. "Do you think my work is dull?" Her disappointment was genuine. So was the devastatingly handsome smile that spread across his face. The hands that were looped loosely behind her, now brought her closer.

"Nothing about you is dull," he said, "except your determination to hold me at arms' length."

Arms' length was a lot farther than where she was now. Well within the circle of his arms, with her hands braced at the point where his jeans met his hips, she was under his spell.

Ross lowered his head and kissed her, tasting the sweetness of her mouth, and it struck her that she might well have been too successful at her own game. By denying the past, she was responding to him in the present alone. Her return kiss was gentle, sampling. She played with being free of all memory, all guilt. Her lips opened to his. She gave of herself as she hadn't done in years.

"That was nice," he whispered against her mouth, then pulled away and set her back before she could do it herself. He trailed a long thumb across her cheek to the lips he'd just left. "We'll do it again soon."

It was said so gently and carried such lightness that Chloe couldn't help but smile. A warm flush painted her cheeks a comely pink, complementing the gray of her eyes, which held a hint of apology. "You have a way of sneaking up when a girl least expects it, Ross. What am I going to do with you?"

His gaze told her first, and there was something heady about it, until he added, "You're going to love me one day. That's what you're going to do." She stiffened, but he went on. "Right now, you're going for a ride with me."

"I have errands to do," she protested.

"Like?"

"Like marketing, for starters. In one meal you've nearly wiped me out."

"So we'll go to the market. What else?"

She ad-libbed. "I need new house plants for the living room. With winter coming on—"

"Winter? It's creeping up toward seventy again today. How can you think of winter?"

"It'll be here. And anyway, the sooner the plants get used to the house, the easier it will be for them to adapt to the cooler weather."

His gaze narrowed. "I bet you talk to your plants."

"No. If I did that, they might think I was flaky. I want my plants to respect me."

She doubted Ross heard her. He was focusing on her mouth, looking entranced. Suddenly he slid the fingers of both hands through the hair on either side of her face, brought his own head down, and kissed her again. This time there was a hunger there hadn't been before, a new urgency. This time Chloe was frightened. How not to lose herself in that hunger?

"Ross," she cried, "don't, please, don't."

He released her. His voice remained husky, but his eyes held a promise. "I won't push you now. But you will love me one day. One day soon."

"You're wrong—"

"Not this time, princess." He paused to let his

breathing steady. "Let's go. We'll stop for lunch first. I'm starved."

Chloe took a steadying breath of her own. "After that breakfast?"

"That breakfast," he grumbled, "was interrupted. And anyway, that was this morning. It's nearly two. Any more feeble excuses to try on me before we leave?"

Chloe looked around her office. Its familiarity gave her strength. Indifference. She could do it.

"Not a one," she said, preceding Ross from the room without another word. It was only when they reached the front door that she felt an odd sense of adventure. Eyes alight, she turned back to Ross. "I have an idea. Let's take the bike."

"I have a better idea," he countered, pulling the neck of his turtleneck away from his skin. "Let's change into cooler things. I hadn't expected it would get so warm."

Assuming that his clothes were still at Lee's house, she felt generous. "Okay. You go back and change. I'll just sit here and—hey! What are you doing?"

It was pretty obvious, actually. With a fast tug he freed his sweater from his jeans, crisscrossed his arms, and smoothly whipped the black turtleneck over his head and off. Never, ever, would Chloe forget that moment when, muscles stretched, his chest came into view.

Lightly bronzed, with a liberal hazing of hair

that tapered toward his navel, it was a solid wall of hard, glorious flesh. Her mouth went dry. She could only stare.

"My bags are right here," he replied, retrieving a soft leather duffel from beside the sofa. Long arms pulled at the duffel's zipper. Deft fingers exchanged the sweater for a lighter, short-sleeved jersey. He quickly drew it over his head. Once more Chloe trembled as that body stretched, flexed, then settled back down, mercifully covered again.

Ross grinned. "There. Easy enough. Do you need to change or anything? Are you cool enough?

Chloe didn't think she would ever be cool enough again. "Uh, I'm fine." She cleared her throat awkwardly, turning and escaping to the wide-open spaces without any further attempt at wit. And she had suggested taking the bike! They would be better off swimming. They might not get to any store, but they would have a barrel of much-needed cold water between them!

But too late. He was at her heels as she led the way to the side shed that housed her motorbike.

"You drive this yourself?" Ross asked, eyeing the small vehicle with something short of trust.

"Sure," she said, praying that he not hear her breathlessness and guess its cause. "It's great for the fresh air, uses practically no gas, and does much less by way of pollution than my car." She paused. "Unless you'd feel safer—"

"No. No. I'm game. Don't forget—of the two of us, I'm the original hippie."

Chloe drove with Ross straddling the seat behind her, and it was totally traumatic. He was near, so near. His arms were locked about her waist, his body tucked against hers. Even the October breeze whipping by did nothing to relieve the intimacy of the trip. When he spoke, it was a nibble at her ear. A nibble? Had he really done that—or was it a product of her overworked imagination?

Indifference. Uh-huh.

The road they traveled was one she covered daily. Its sides were edged with maples and oaks, grown ripe and mellow now, on the verge of bursting into autumn flame. Fields sprawled to the right, wooded pastureland to the left. Ahead undulated a path to Sakonnet Point, the very tip of the finger of land on which Little Compton sat just across the bay from Newport.

If Ross was aware of the havoc his nearness wreaked on her, he kept his smugness in check. Once, in a gesture of soft intimacy, he released her waist to gather her hair together in his hands, twist the long fall once, and tuck it inside the back of her shirt.

"The better to see the town," he murmured wickedly. He had to know that her neck tingled from the touch of those fingers, her ear from the brush of his breath, so much so that she was oblivious to much of their surroundings. When at last they reached the wharf, with its graceful fleet of pleasure craft, she was almost sorry. The intimacy had been nice. She was strangely torn.

Not so Ross. "Ah! There's a place that looks like it'll fit the bill. Can we eat there?"

The ultimate humiliation had to be being bested by a restaurant. Apparently the way to a man's heart was through his stomach after all. But then, Chloe wanted no part of Ross's heart. The restaurant could have him.

She smiled, pleased to have so neatly talked herself sane. "If you're really hungry, this is the place to be."

Ross was really hungry. He was game to sample most anything and everything, from clam fritters to little necks on the half shell to swordfish puffs, a specialty of the house.

Chloe savored his enthusiasm, taking pride in pointing out the small groups of local fishermen on the pier arduously scraping barnacles off tall-stacked lobster traps. The bright yellow of their rubber overalls was a bit of sunshine stolen from the sky, adding a spark to the otherwise sleepy air of the harbor. It was, all in all, a peaceful lunch, filled with good food, thirst-quenching beer, and conversation that stuck to the more general, less personal topic of travels, foreign ports, and favorite hideaways.

"The ocean is beautiful," Ross admitted at one point, "but I still prefer the mountains. There's nothing more lovely than that feeling of seclusion you get in a small cabin tucked into a neat cleft, with stretches and stretches of piggybacked hills to keep the world at bay."

"Then you've never been on the beach on a foggy morning," Chloe returned softly. "It's like being in a gentle white cocoon, with the solace of knowing that humanity is near, yet out of sight and sound for as long as the mist should choose."

"You like New England."

"I do."

"You'll be staying here?"

"I will."

He sighed good-naturedly. "Then we'd better get you to the market or you won't make it through the week, much less the winter."

On that comfortable note, they left the restaurant, spending leisurely moments wandering along the breakwater before returning to the bike.

"I'll drive this time," Ross said with an arched brow and a palm out for the keys. Chloe was only too glad to relinquish the responsibility. Seated comfortably behind Ross, she was more in control of her emotions.

What she hadn't counted on was the broad

expanse of his back, the sense of contentment that flowed through her as the wind rushed freely through her hair, the gentle fatigue that a night of little sleep, a morning of busy work, and a full stomach had induced. Indifference had no place here. Without a care to the wisdom of the move, she wrapped her arms about his middle and laid her cheek against his back.

It was heaven, pure and simple. She didn't have a care in the world. Ross was at the helm, competent and strong. Over the wind that sailed by came the steady beat of his heart, steadying her in turn. She didn't know what it was about this particular man that affected her so deeply, nor did she care just then. It was enough to enjoy the respite from responsibility and to give herself up to his care, if only for the brief ride home.

The brief ride home, however, grew longer and longer. Peering around Ross's shoulder, Chloe saw that they were on a different road entirely.

"Do you know where we are?" she called.

"Roughly. Where's your market?"

He followed her pointing finger, turning this way, then that, until the town common came into view. Typically New England, it had a white-steepled church at its hub and a variety of rural shops and boutiques. Chloe found everything she needed at the grocery store, reluctantly took Ross's suggestion that the plants be saved for another trip, then climbed behind him onto the bike to return to the house. Not one wrong turn later she was on her own front steps.

The moment of reckoning was at hand. "Will you be returning to New York now?" she asked.

He had finished stowing the bike in its proper spot and advanced on her with a grin. Relieving her of the large brown bag she'd been carrying, he took her elbow and guided her toward the house. "Not yet."

"You're going back to Lee's?"

"Not yet."

"Then what are you going to do?"

He held the door open for her to pass, and followed her into the kitchen, where he began to unload and store the groceries as though the place were his. "I want to make a few phone calls." He glanced at his watch. "Then wash the car, catch the end of the Giants' game, shower and shave, and take you out to dinner."

His recitation was so nonchalant that Chloe would have guessed he spent every October Saturday this way, at least as far as the first part went. As for taking her out to dinner, it had certainly never happened before.

"It's unnecessary," she said.

"Which part—the calls, the car, the game, or the shower?"

"The dinner! Lunch was enough to even us up.

There's no need for anything more."

A muscle worked in Ross's jaw. "It's not tit-for-tat, Chloe. I'd like to take you out to dinner."

"I appreciate the thought, but—"

"No buts. We're going out for dinner. Period."

"What if I have other plans?"

He arched a dark brow. "Do you?"

"I could just as well," she hedged, "for the way you just assume I'm free."

"Well, are you?"

It wasn't that she didn't want to go to dinner with Ross. On the contrary. She liked being with him. She just didn't want to get used to it.

"Chloe?"

"Yes," she said, sighing. "I'm free."

"Good. Say, about eight?"

"But—"

"Eight it is. And Chloe?"

She felt totally helpless. "What?"

"How about if we dress up?"

"Dress up? I haven't 'dressed up' in months. Things here are very casual. There's nowhere—"

"There is," he argued gently. "Leave that to me."

Chloe lowered her eyes and studied the floor, then slowly shook her head. "Ross, I'd really rather—"

"For old times' sake?" he dared ask. "Today we played 'far out.' Tonight, let's play 'far in.' Come on. How about it? Just this once?"

The odd note of pleading in his voice brought Chloe's head slowly up. He looked so innocent, so hopeful, that she couldn't turn him down.

"Just this once," she gave in softly, forcing the semblance of a smile to vulnerable lips.

There was no semblance of anything in Ross's smile. It was blatantly broad and open, relieved and pleased. It warmed her, reassured her, amused her. And it most definitely excited her.

That terrified her.

Before she could back out, though, he said, "It's a date. See you at eight."

He turned and made for the phone, leaving Chloe to gather the pieces of her fast-splintering resolve and struggle with makeshift repairs before evening rolled around.

6

It wasn't an easy task. Ross seemed to be every-where she turned. He used her office to make his calls, lounging back in her chair, legs long and straight, crossed lazily at the ankles, propped on the corner of her desk. His presence filled the room so that it took a conscious effort on Chloe's part to quietly creep in and steal her own work. He followed her every move with interest, though he was at the same time maddeningly capable of car-rying on his end of what was obviously a business discussion.

After retreating to the back porch to bask in the rays of the westward sun, she put her best effort into organizing the papers on her lap. But her best effort was sadly lacking. Her mind wan-dered. Then Ross appeared in the flesh to ask about a bucket, a sponge, and some old towels. He was right on schedule, his self-satisfied air announced. He vanished, then reappeared and deposited the car-wash gear on the sandy grass beside the very same porch on which she sat.

Would he do it here? she wondered. The smooth hum of his car's engine as he pulled the vehicle close by the side of the house was her answer. He wanted an audience, the rat.

She should have gotten up and left, but she sat right there in the large wood-slatted porch chair, watching while he put his best effort into washing, drying, and polishing his sporty brown BMW. As he stretched to soap the roof, the muscles of his shoulders bunched. When he squatted to scrub the whitewalls, the muscles of his thighs swelled. When he reached across the front windshield, his shirt separated from his jeans, giving fleeting, devastating glimpses of a flat, hard belly. And through it all was the sight of hands and forearms at work, lightly tanned, softly haired.

When Chloe had taken as much as she could, she stacked her papers into a pile, left the chair, and, without a word to explain her sudden departure, went into the house. To clean? She hated to clean! How else, though, to expend some of the nervous energy that had gathered inside?

She swept the floors and vacuumed the carpets, all at doublespeed, all with every bit of elbow grease she could muster. Tables, chairs, countertops, and shelves met similar fates beneath her dustcloth. Perspiration beaded on her upper lip. She barely noticed.

The football game offered a different torment, but one that was no less agonizing. She was polishing the aged oak banister halfway to the second floor when the familiar sound wafted up, and she sank down on the homey wool runner in defeat. The football game—what memories it brought. That sound—the excited roar of the crowd, the babble of color commentators, the endless streams of kickoffs and passes, punts and first downs, fumbles, tumbles, and pileups—brought back the days in New Orleans when the men of the family gathered for their weekly fix. Her brothers—it had been so long since she'd seen them. Were they watching this same game? And how was her father feeling? He wasn't young anymore. Should she make the effort to go back before . . . ?

"Chloe? Are you all right?"

It wasn't until Ross spoke that she realized he'd even approached. Nor had she been aware of the tears in her eyes. With a hard swallow and a feeble smile, she willed the sadness away. "I'm fine. I think I'll go for a run."

Leaving Ross where he stood, she pensively covered the last of the steps to the top landing, disappeared into her room to change into running wear, then went back down the stairs and outside. Her sneakers beat rhythmically down the beach toward the far end of the bay, much as they had done at roughly the same time the day before. Had it only been twenty-four hours since Ross had shown up? Already he seemed so at home here. Worse, at odd times it seemed natural to have him here.

The questions kept pace with her jog. Was it only that Ross was a face from her past? Was he a link to those people who had once meant so much to her? Did she crave the warmth of her family? Was Ross, by association, an extension of them?

Without answers, she paced herself for another ten minutes before turning around. When she reached the house she didn't bother to stop at the door. An easy lope carried her into the kitchen, through to the living room, and up the stairs. No sign of Ross—so much the better. Jogging in place with the last of her pre-shower energy, she piled her arms with fresh towels from a surprisingly low stack in the linen closet and went to her room for a robe. There she stopped dead in her tracks.

Where an open expanse of pale lavender quilt had been when she had left, was a landscape of male artifacts. And clothes. His clothes. He had made himself perfectly at home. This was the limit.

A fit of fury took her to the bathroom door. Better judgment stopped her on the threshold. The sink taps were running. If she barged in, what would she find? The tremble that snaked through her had nothing to do with fear. Rather, she conjured up the image of Ross shaving, a coat of white lather covering his jaw, a towel—her towel—covering his loins, and nothing, nothing else, covering or covered.

As she stood rooted there, the shower went on, the curtain curtain clattered back on its hooks, and . . . her mind's eye saw it all. The towel fell away. With total nonchalance, he stepped into the shower.

Mercifully, he couldn't hear her low cry as she whirled back toward her bedroom, cursing both Ross and her imagination all the way. But she couldn't curb her curiosity entirely. Approaching the bed with an odd shyness, she studied his things. There was the leather duffel she had seen earlier, plus a larger, flatter suit bag, unzipped to reveal a pair of gray-blue tweed lapels. There was the smaller canvas case that had contained his shaving gear, if the travel-sized bottle of cologne left behind was any indication. There was a shirt—white, freshly laundered, lightly starched. There were a tie, clean socks, shorts—

"Oh, Lord!" she exclaimed softly. If every stitch of the clothing he intended to put on was here on her bed, exactly what did he plan to wear for the trip from the bathroom?

Anticipation constricted her throat, making breathing harder. The aftereffects of her jog had faded; this quickening was due to desire. Ross turned her on. Part of her wanted nothing more than to give herself to him. Give herself? Hah! She would take as well, take as she had been too naive to do eleven years before. She felt suddenly greedy, possessed with a need to satisfy the gnawing inside.

"You're back!"

Chloe whirled around.

Undaunted by her alarm, he grinned. "I'd hoped to be out of your way." He gestured in token apology toward her bed. "Guess I misjudged the time." He shot a look at the hall. "I helped myself to your supplies. That okay?"

That okay? The towel was draped around his hips with as much panache—and as little cere-mony—as she had earlier imagined. It hung low on his stomach and left little to the imagination. She dragged her eyes upward, following a narrow line of hair past his navel to his waist and slowly higher.

"Chloe," Ross began in husky chiding, "do you have any idea what it does to a man when a woman looks at him that way?"

It took every ounce of her willpower to keep from lowering her gaze in curiosity. "I'm sorry—"

"Oh, don't be sorry." He came closer. Though he didn't touch her, his body was no more than a breath away.

And she felt it, felt the need. She put a hand to his chest to ward it off, but it was a sorry miscalculation. Her fingers found a mat of soft, dark hair that sprang, warm and still moist, from the freshness of lightly bronzed skin.

The pounding of her pulse frightened her so that she tore her hand from his chest and thrust it behind her back. She felt a huge measure of guilt. If he did also, it was hidden behind desire. His amber eyes smoldered, heating her all the more. The need, ahhhh, the need. The ache to be held and loved . . .

Ever so slowly, Ross lowered his head until his lips shadowed hers. She felt them, wanted them. Her own parted in silent invitation. She closed her eyes to savor the sensation. But he never kissed her. Rather, there was a soft exchange of breath, a whisper of lips against one another, sweet, sweet torment.

Chloe felt ready to burst, willing to beg. But that was a sure road to self-disgust. So she finally did what she had meant to do all along. She pressed against his chest, pushing him gently but firmly away.

As he slowly straightened to what was, even barefoot, an awesome height, he cleared his throat. "You'd better wait downstairs," he said in a voice that was thick and taut. "I'll finish up quickly."

She took his suggestion. By the time she reached the bottommost step, sanity had fully returned. Swearing softly, she traipsed through the kitchen and stood on the back porch looking out on the beach. But the tide within her was high. No amount of cooling breeze could stem it.

He had to leave. It was as simple as that. Indifference was a pipe dream. He stirred her too much.

Having him around today was a taste of what it might be like to have him around all the time. She wanted to say she had hated it, but she couldn't. There had been something nice about waking to find a man in her kitchen cooking her breakfast, something nice about knowing that he was patiently waiting for her to finish work, something nice about going marketing with him, even about finding him in her shower. It had been nice. But would any man fit the bill?

With a sigh, she shook her head. It had to be Ross. Always Ross.

"It's all yours, princess!" he called.

Chloe looked up in surprise to find the horizon pink-orange in advance of sunset. Back over her shoulder, Ross stood at the kitchen door, silhouetted by the light inside.

"Be right there," she called, looking at the sunset again, gathering composure. When she felt in control, she returned to the house. She caught a trace of cologne when she moved past him, but moved steadily on until she was safe in her room.

*   *   *

Promptly at eight she descended the stairs, wearing a pale blue sheath of lightweight wool appropriate to the fast-cooling night air. Its lines were simple; it was nipped in at the waist and wrists, lightly flared at the sleeves and skirt, and deeply slashed into a vee at the throat.

She worried about that low vee. The dress was simple, but provocative. She had bought it the year before for one of those blundered attempts at a date, and would have avoided it for that reason. Unfortunately, it was the only dressy dress in her wardrobe that was of recent vintage.

In other respects she felt confident. Her hair was brushed to a fine sheen, swept back behind either ear, and held in place with buds of pale blue silk. The single pearl at each ear matched the strand around her throat. And her eyes were luminescent. From her makeup, perhaps? Whatever, she felt like a porcelain princess descending the stairs.

Ross was clearly pleased. "You look lovely," he said, gently taking her arm.

She felt suddenly shy. "Where are we going?"

"Farmington Court."

She caught her breath. "In Newport? How did you ever get reservations?"

"Oh, I managed," he said with a coy grin.

Chloe's excitement was genuine. "They've only had the dining room open a few months."

"You haven't eaten there yet, then? I was hoping I'd be the first to take you."

"You are," she said and tried to get a handle on her breathiness. "I usually eat in, remember? No, I haven't eaten at the Court, but I've wanted to. I heard that the dining room is gorgeous and the food incredible." She arched a brow. "You are hungry, aren't you?"

Ross smiled. "Since we're dining in style, I'll try not to paw through the pâté." He tossed his head toward the door. "Let's go."

The drive to the farm took them in a large U, from one fingertip of land, back to the mainland, then out to the other fingertip. Their conversation was light, in contrast to the heavy darkness that had fallen. Even the moon had disappeared behind gathering clouds.

Chloe was vitally aware of Ross. His strapping presence filled the car and her senses, adding to her excitement.

Farmington Court was on the outskirts of Newport. Without any help from Chloe, Ross found the place with ease.

"How did you find out about the Court?" she asked when the farm appeared on a gentle rise ahead. "Not many people know about the dining room here. Not many outsiders, that is. It's a well-kept secret."

His smile reflected the bright lights of the house. "Maybe it's supposed to be a secret, but it's slowly creeping out anyway. I had a recommendation from a friend in New York who's been here." He paused, then confessed, "I'm not a total stranger to Newport. Little Compton, yes. Newport, no. I was here last summer."

"You were?" she asked cautiously.

He nodded. "I spent several days here sailing with friends."

"I didn't know you sailed."

"There's plenty you don't know about me." With a flick of his wrist, he turned the car into a space in the graveled lot. He slid from behind the wheel, rounded the car, and helped her out.

She learned something else about him when they passed through the door of the sprawling seaside estate. Not only did he greet the maître d' by name, but he spoke in fluent French. Along with her Southern accent, Chloe had long since lost what little French she picked up as a child in New Orleans. She remained silent, enjoying the smooth, romantic sound.

Following several moments of low conversation during which both men seemed equally at ease, the maître d' showed Ross and Chloe to the smallest of the three rooms that had been converted for public dining. It was exquisitely decorated in Colonial style, with a smattering of the English, a dab of the French, and a triumphant dose of pure Americana. This particular room held only three tables, each set for two. Theirs was in a far corner, lit softly by a candle. It was an intimate setting, one Chloe would have wished to avoid had she been thinking clearly.

But she wasn't. At some point Ross had ceased to be a part of the past. There was only the candlelit present. She looked over the flickering flame and met his gaze.

"Do you like it?" he asked, endearingly eager.

She smiled. "I do."

"I asked the maître d' to bring a bottle of Chassagne de Montrachet."

If his fluency in French amazed her, his knowledge of fine wines was no less astonishing. Fine wines were something she did know something about, a legacy of her father's acclaimed cellar. Unable to resist, she grinned. "So that's how the Army sedates its brats. Fine wine. And here I felt so sorry for you. I'm sure the Chassagne de Montrachet will be superb."

Ross laughed. "The Army had nothing to do with it. I developed a taste for wine after I left the Peace Corps. I have several treasured bottles at home—a Mouton-Rothschild, a Château Lafite-Rothschild. My favorite is a 1959 Côteaux du Layon from the Loire Valley."

"Whoa. Very impressive. What other goodies do you have up your sleeve?"

His right hand flew to his left cuff, one long finger making a pretense of searching. The search was forgotten when the maître d' reappeared, wine in hand, to present the bottle to Ross.

While he studied the wine, Chloe studied him. It was a luxury that the drive through the night hadn't offered. Now she drank in his good looks with as much reverence as he gave to his wine.

He looked wonderful. His suit was the gray-blue tweed she had seen on the bed. Same with his white shirt and crimson-on-navy tie. She blushed as she recalled the other items she'd seen, then pushed those aside and focused on the chiseled features before her. They were strong, yet relaxed, and exuded confidence. The darkness of his hair and the sun-touched hue of his skin contrasted with his shirt at neck and wrists, adding a crispness to his appearance that was enhanced by the fine cut of the obviously hand-tailored fabric. He was the epitome of the man of the world—suave, assured, experienced, and content. To all outward appearances he held the world in his palm.

Was he vulnerable in any way?

"Why the frown, princess?" He leaned forward to exclude the maître d', who worked at uncorking the wine.

"I'm not frowning." But she was. She felt it. "I

was wondering . . ." When the maître d' poured a sip of wine into Ross's glass and waited, Chloe held the thought.

Ross lifted the long-stemmed goblet, inhaled the scent, took the pale liquid into his mouth, patiently let his taste buds warm it, finally swallowed. "Excellent," he complimented the very pleased maître d'. Without further fanfare the goblets, first Chloe's, then Ross's, were filled.

"What were you wondering?" Ross asked the instant they were alone again.

"Whether you're happy. Are you content with your life?"

"For the most part. There are still things I want." The directness of his gaze should have tipped her off.

But she was too curious to see. The softness of her voice spread to her lips, now moist with wine. "What things?"

"You hit on them yesterday, actually. I want a wife and children."

"But you've waited this long."

"Not by choice."

"Then why?"

His crooked grin did stranger things inside her than even the wine, with its gentle warming touch. "I'm not totally different from that man back in New Orleans. I'm an idealist at heart. I always will be. I have a certain image of what love should be like. If I can't have it that way, I'd rather not have it at all."

Chloe looked down. What was love? What would she have wanted from it had she allowed it into her life? She watched Ross's fingers, curling absently around his goblet's stem. At that moment, love would have meant reaching out to touch them, to thread hers through them.

Burying her hand in her lap, she said, "Tell me about that image, Ross. In its most ideal form, what should love be like?"

He stared at her, his eyes a pensive gold. He seemed to weigh and balance, to sift through both sides of a private debate as the quiet sounds of the restaurant drifted by.

Chloe waited, sipping wine, buoyed by it. Her thoughts wandered, but not in debate. There was nothing to debate. Ross Stephenson was even more appealing than he had been in her memory all those years. He was a man for today, to be sipped and savored like the wine he poured into her now empty glass.

When he spoke, she was grateful for the wine's mellowing shield. "When was the last time you were home?"

"Home?"

"New Orleans. Do you go back there often?"

"No." New Orleans was the past. She wanted the present. "What does that have to do with anything?"

"Love. You asked me about it. I'm asking you the same. You loved your family once. Do you still?"

"Yes."

"But you never see them. Don't you miss them?"

Even in spite of the wine, she grew defensive. "I do."

"How often do you call home?" he asked gently.

"Every so often."

"And the last time you flew down?"

She hedged. "It was a while ago."

When he leaned forward to pursue his point, she sensed that he really and truly cared. "Why, Chloe? What does love mean to you that you can ignore those same people who worry themselves sick about you? That can't be what love is about."

"We're talking about different kinds of love. One kind you're born into, the other you choose."

"The end result is the same. Once a man and a woman make that commitment and marry, they face the same kinds of trials that your family faced. You've run away—"

"Don't." She clamped a hand on his arm. "Please don't, Ross. I don't want to talk about this."

His voice gentled. "You have to talk about it sometime. There are so many things you've refused to face, about yourself, about your family—"

"Not tonight," she insisted softly. She let her

eyes plead, only because her voice kept its dignity. "I want to enjoy myself tonight. Please?"

Ross stared first at her, then at the tablecloth, then at the far wall. When his gaze finally returned she saw a glint of humor. "When you look at me like that, I'd do anything!"

"Anything?" She clutched at that.

"Anything."

"Then tell me about the Picasso exhibit. You saw it when it was in New York, didn't you? Was it as spectacular as the reviews claimed?"

"Every bit."

She waited for him to say more, but he simply stared at her.

"Go on, Ross. Tell me about it."

His gaze narrowed. "I'm not giving up, Chloe. We'll get back to that other conversation sooner or later. For now I'll humor you."

"I'm waiting," she sang brightly, making light of his threat. "The exhibit?"

The evening passed more quickly than she could have dreamed. Not only did they discuss Picasso, but they delved into politics, Wall Street, and the National Football League as well. For Chloe, the Châteaubriand Bouquetière with Béarnaise Sauce was incidental, as was the mellow red wine that flowed with the appearance of the beef. Her attention was on Ross and Ross alone.

When was it that she had vowed indifference? That morning? What a fool she had been to think she could remain indifferent to Ross for long. She knew her eyes were sparkling and her cheeks flushed, and she couldn't seem to stop smiling. Indifferent? Fat chance. Even aside from the physical, she found him to be the most interesting, well-informed, articulate man she had ever known. Though they didn't agree on everything, he respected Chloe's right to her own opinion. It made conversation free and relaxed, neither one fearful of offending the other.

The blend of Ross and the wine put Chloe at ease. When he suggested that they take dessert cheese home to eat with fruit overlooking the ocean, she was all for it. Unfortunately, it was downright chilly when they emerged from Farmington Court, and it began to drizzle during the drive home.

"So much for a gentle evening breeze," Ross grumbled as he hustled Chloe up the front steps to her door between increasingly large drops of rain. "The living room will have to do."

"That'll be fine. I'm in the mood for Debussy anyway, and it would have competed with the surf."

He smiled at her. *"La Mer?"*

"I had another of his works in mind." Once inside, she went straight to the shelves below the stereo unit, where she kept a small but cherished collection of works of the masters. With pride she pulled one CD from the lot.

Ross's brow shot up. *"L'Après-midi d'un faune?"* Again his accent was flawless. "I haven't listened to that in years!"

"I always called it *Afternoon of a Faun.* I like the way you say it, though. It sounds so much more romantic."

"It is a romantic piece."

Ignoring the note of caution that sounded from somewhere in the back of her mind, she took out the CD. The entire evening had been romantic, so why not this? If she was enjoying herself, why stop?

Ross squatted to study her collection. His expression was all male and distinctly wicked when he winked back over his shoulder. "You have Ravel. Should I put that on?"

She had seen that video, too. "Debussy will be fine," she said without batting an eyelash.

Richly pictorial chords filled the room. Chloe sank into a corner of the sofa, put her head back, and closed her eyes. She was aware of movement within the room, but concentrated on the music floating softly through the air about her. She was dreaming, wakened only by the warm lips that kissed her bare throat once. Her eyes flew open.

"Come sit with me and have some cheese." He took her hand and coaxed her to the floor beside a plate of cheese and fruit. She slipped off her high-heeled sandals.

They sat in front of the sofa and chairs, on the thick cream-colored area rug that covered the hardwood floor. Chloe was the keeper of the edibles, slicing fruit and cheese, stacking a piece of one on the other to offer Ross. He lounged casually on an elbow, legs stretched and crossed as he kept their wineglasses filled.

"Are you trying to get me drunk?" she teased.

"What fun would you be drunk?" He paused. "Are you sure you don't want to listen to Ravel?"

"Don't you like Debussy?" she asked innocently. Ross simply topped off her wineglass.

In the hours that followed they talked more. Chloe asked Ross about his childhood and discovered that he had both a sister and a brother, that he had studied the violin during one of his mother's culture binges, and that he had been expelled from school for a day after tossing a water bomb from a second-story building and soaking kids in the playground.

"A water bomb? Ross, how could you? That's the type of thing the girls always hated!"

"That's why I did it."

"Come on," she chided, her eyes half closed, "a ladies' man like you?"

"Sure. I was eight at the time. It satisfied my need for machismo."

Chloe laughed at the idea of an eight-year-old Ross striving for machismo. He certainly didn't need to strive now.

"You have three brothers, don't you?" Ross picked the perfect time to turn the conversation. She was in a more relaxed, more open mood than earlier. It didn't occur to her not to answer.

"Uh-huh. Allan, Chris, and Tim. They've gone into Daddy's business." She frowned. "I haven't seen them in a while."

"Will you be going down for Thanksgiving next month?"

November was the last time of year she ever went to visit. "No. I think Tim will be in New York then. I may meet him there. I'm not sure. I haven't heard from him in a while."

"Do you call them?"

This time, she did smell the trap. "Oh, no, you don't, Ross Stephenson. I'm not so tipsy that I can't see what you're doing. It won't work."

"You won't tell me about you?" he asked with such honest disappointment that she almost gave in. Almost, but not quite. There was too much she didn't want to face tonight. This was a night for the present. She shook her head in silent insistence.

"Then sit closer." Before she could protest he had shifted so that she leaned against him as he leaned against the sofa. "There." His voice was pleasantly husky. "Comfortable?"

"Ummm." She was extremely so. In fact, she couldn't think of a place where she would have been more comfortable. Ross's chest was broad under her cheek, his arms were gentle around her, his heart beat a pacifying tattoo through her.

Time became an expendable entity; there was no need to move. They sat quietly in one another's arms, lulled by the music that continued to play. Debussy had long since given way to Grieg and Tchaikovsky.

Given the wine, the song, and the man, Chloe was mellow. So she had no problem when Ross said, "You and Crystal were identical, weren't you?"

"Technically, but there were differences we could see."

His breath rustled the hair at her temple. "Were you inseparable as kids?"

"Pretty much. Since the guys were a lot older than we were, there were only the two of us around the house."

"You had a built-in playmate."

"Uh-huh. It was fun. She was the more adventurous. I was the more conservative."

"But you were the one who approached me that night, not Crystal. I always wondered why."

Chloe tipped her head back to look at him. "We argued about who you were looking at. I thought it was me. Crystal said you wouldn't see the difference." She paused. "Who were you looking at, Ross? Me, or Crystal?"

His lips curved gently, tickling her nose for an instant. "You both looked the same."

"We did not. Come on, which one was it?" Her teasing was gentle, but she needed to know.

Ross raised his eyes. "Ah, let me think. There was one with dark hair curled to the left, and one with dark hair curled to—"

She pinched his ribs. "I'm serious! Or were you just interested in any pretty girl?"

He sobered then. "I wanted you, Chloe. I saw the difference. Your sister was just as lovely, but you had something more. I can't quite explain it."

He didn't have to. Knowing that he had chosen her was enough to ease part of that guilt she had felt over the years.

He tightened his arms. "Okay, princess. Now you tell me. Why were you the one who came forward?"

"I wanted you more."

When he sucked in a breath Chloe's hand slid lower on his abdomen. On dangerous ground, she raised it to the point where his tie lay in a loose knot, where the top two buttons of his shirt were released. His chest beckoned. She touched it and found it wonderfully warm.

Ross's voice grew thicker. "You argued?"

"Not exactly."

"If Crystal was the more impulsive of the two, I can't believe she gave up without a fight."

"I wouldn't call it a fight."

"Then what? What settled it?"

Chloe was suddenly unsure. What they had done sounded crass. But she had come this far. "We, uh, we tossed a coin."

"Excuse me?"

"We tossed a coin."

"To see which one of you would get me?" At her nod he burst into a laugh. "Chloe MacDaniel! I'm appalled! You mean to tell me that you let the toss of a coin decide whether you or your sister would seduce me? That's awful!"

She leaned closer, whispered, "It wasn't a fair toss." Tempted headily by the male tang of his skin, she kissed his chest.

"Excuse me?"

She cleared her throat. "I knew I would win."

Ross held her back, staring in bemusement. "Explain, please."

"Crystal and I used to play tricks on one another. We each had our strong points. She always beat me when it came to motivating herself. She was the first to get behind the wheel of the car, the first to choose the prettiest dress in the boutique, the first to snag the telephone caller. I prided myself on being the clever one."

"And this coin toss?"

Chloe begged forgiveness with her eyes. "It was my coin. I called heads."

Understanding slowly dawned on Ross's face. His grin was appreciative. "And the coin had two heads?"

"It did."

Whatever he might have thought of her for having cheated, he was undoubtedly pleased that "winning" him had meant so much to her. "That deserves a kiss," he said and lowered his head.

7

Chloe met his lips without hesitation. She had waited for this all evening. They had been building toward it from the second she had agreed to dress up and go out to dinner with him. "Just this once," she had told him then. Now the words echoed through her. Just this once she would relax in Ross's arms. Just this once she would taste his love. Just this once she would be free of the past.

She'd had too much wine. No doubt about that. Would she want this if her head were clear? Maybe yes, maybe no, but it made no difference. Right here, right now, she was where she wanted to be.

Ross appeared equally content, if the leisure of his kiss meant anything. He tasted her again and again, seeming to find something new each time. She sure did. Once it was the sweetness of wine on his lips, another time the firmness of his mouth, another the heat. His kiss was a heady brew, warm, moist, and intoxicating.

Seeking more, she spread her hands over his

chest and discovered a textured surface beneath the smoothness of his shirt. He was a man of many layers to be explored, one by one. She was the explorer, on an ocean of desire, clinging to him as to a raft on a rising sea of sensation.

His tongue sought and caressed, sucking hers deeper, sparking greater response, and she gave it unconditionally, opening to him in delight. Soft sighs were breathed and swallowed, one mouth to the other.

The urgency built. Just when she needed it, he deepened the kiss. His lips controlled hers now, as did the hands that framed her face.

His voice was thick against her mouth. "Do you have any idea what you do to me?"

Her answer was a breathy, "I know what you do to me. It happens every time."

"Does it? It's been a long time since you were with a man."

"By choice. By choice." Tipping her head back on his shoulder, she studied his strong jaw, straight nose, amber eyes. "It was never a trial for me before. I've never really wanted another man."

"Is it a trial now?" he whispered, momentarily cautious. "What do you want, Chloe? Do you know?"

She answered by dipping her head and putting her lips to his throat. Intoxicated by its musky scent, she freed the knot of his tie and released the front buttons of his shirt. Her sigh warmed him when her hands slid over his flesh, but his moan prevented her from going on.

He pushed his hands into her hair. "Look at me!" His eyes were hot with desire. "Do you know what I want, Chloe? I want to feel you. I want to know every inch of your body. Half measures never worked for me with you. I need to be inside you. Can you accept that?" His gaze flickered over her flushed features. "Will you hate yourself tomorrow?"

The question took her by surprise. She didn't want to think about tomorrow. Her eyes filled with the tears of a deep, emotional yearning. "I don't know what I'll feel tomorrow, but I know what I want now. I know what I need."

"Why now?" It was another surprise question. "Eleven years ago it was rebellion."

"Not rebellion."

"Then why?" he asked more gently.

She took a deep breath. The scent of his skin gave her strength. "Yes, you were different. The other men we'd known had been handpicked. Our brothers were as fussy as our parents. But there was more for me. You were new. Refreshing."

"A challenge?"

"Maybe."

"Do I challenge you now?"

"Yes, but that's only part of it." Need loosened

her tongue. "The pull is there, just like it was eleven years ago. Don't make me try to explain it, because I can't. Lord only knows I didn't want to feel anything for you! You were the one who showed up uninvited, remember?"

He smiled dryly. "So you've told me."

"You bring back memories. Maybe what I need is to wipe out those memories with new ones."

His smile turned wry. "You are using me."

When Chloe pushed herself up, his hands fell away. She was on her own, as she had been all those years. And she knew what she wanted.

"Yes, I'm using you! I'm using you to show me that I can feel and live. I'm using you to help me put the past to rest. You're right. I have to do that. But don't you see," she ended on a note of pleading, "that you're the only one who can help me?"

For long moments, silence was as thick in the air as the lingering heat of passion. Finally Ross lifted a hand to her cheek. "I want to believe it, Chloe. Want it bad."

"Then make love to me. You show me what love should be like."

With a low animal sound, he reached out and pulled her under him, kissing her fiercely, erasing everything but the here and now. Chloe put herself into his hands. Trusting him fully, she lost all inhibition and returned his kiss with everything she had.

His lips moved on her neck, inching down into the dip of her dress. "I've been wanting to do this all night," he whispered moments before his mouth found the bottommost point. He kissed her there, wet, open-mouthed, then rose again. His mouth was ready when he cupped her breasts and lifted them there.

Chloe sighed softly. She squeezed her eyes shut, buried her fingers in his hair, and held him closer.

With excruciating slowness he drew back her bodice, freeing her breast bit by bit. Her insides quivered when her nipple was bared. His breath was hot, the air cool. Arching closer, she watched his tongue touch the pebbled tip, circle it, touch it again.

"Ross!" she gasped, straining beneath him, needing more.

"Love is torment, Chloe. It's wanting and wanting and wanting until you would do anything to get. Be patient."

She tried, but it was a torment, indeed, to watch him pull his shirt from his pants and release every single last button. She bit her lip to keep from reaching out to touch him. He could have been sculpted in clay by a master, he was that beautiful, more beautiful even because he was real. He was human, manly, alive.

Her patience was pushed even further when he drew her up, reached behind to slide her zipper to her waist, then pulled her dress down, easing her arms from their sleeves. Bare to the waist, she needed his touch, but his eyes caressed her first. Her breasts swelled, begging to be cupped and held.

"They're not the same," she whispered falteringly. "I was much younger then."

A sound came from deep in his throat. It gave credence to his words. "Maybe younger then, but better now." His eyes said it was true. With trembling hands, he palmed her breasts with such soft, gentle motion that she nearly cried out again.

Patience slipped slowly away. When she thought she'd seen the last of it, Ross drew her to him, crushing her breasts against his chest in a move that stole her breath.

He made another deep sound, this one very male, very satisfied. His hands moved over her back, covering every inch of its smooth surface, and Chloe followed his lead. Eyes closed, she savored the feel of him, letting her palms play on his back, then drawing away to glory in his chest. His nipples were as flat and hard as hers were raised and swollen. His neck was as strong as hers was slender. His skin was as tanned as hers was creamy. Their bodies were so different, but the light in his eyes matched that in hers. She saw desire there. It was hot and heavy.

Chloe could barely breathe, much less speak.

She was as aroused as she had ever been, and more with each touch of his fingers or tongue. The beat of her heart skipped rapidly on, driving heated blood through her veins. She was free. She was alive. She wanted to belong to Ross then more than anything in the world.

Sensing her urgency, he pulled her up. As she stood, her dress slid past her hips to form a pale blue circle on the floor. Aware of the admiration in his eyes, she stepped out of it wearing nothing but a pair of small silk panties.

When he held out his arms, she went to him and wrapped hers tightly around his neck. Her breasts were crushed against his hairy chest. She burned from within.

"Chloe ... Chloe ... Chloe ..." he chanted softly, reminiscent of that soft September breeze in New Hampshire. But she couldn't think back, not with his fingers skimming her hips, then moving up her sides and around. He was exquisitely tender. She felt cherished, desired, and loved, if only for the night.

"Hurry." She arched against him, her body aflame with need. "Hurry."

Setting her back, he unbuckled his belt and undid his pants. His eyes devoured her hungrily as he pushed everything off, then knelt to remove her panties.

She was trembling with excitement when he

dragged a cushion from the sofa to the floor. He lowered himself and held out a hand, and for a minute she couldn't move, couldn't take her eyes from his body. It was perfect in every way, thoroughly masculine and fully aroused. Eleven years ago she had been too shy to study him, but she wasn't now. He seemed to stretch forever, one long limb connected to another by firm sinew. Had she been an artist she would have drawn him. But she was only a woman.

"Chloe?"

She took his hand and stretched out against him with a soft moan. He felt wonderful against her. When she began to touch him, he sucked in a breath.

"Oh, God," he whispered gruffly, "oh, God, that's it." His chest rose and fell, lungs labored. "Feel it, princess?"

There were two kinds of feeling, the physical and the emotional. Chloe experienced both. High on the fullness, she moved freely over his body. Her fingers found delight with every touch, her heart satisfaction. She reached his most electric parts as he reached for her.

"Now," she begged, desperate and demanding.

"Kiss me first," he murmured thickly. When she turned up her face, he moved over her, slipping between her open thighs.

She cried into his mouth when he thrust forward. Anything she might have remembered of the past was gone then, paling in the light of the present. Her body exploded and flamed, burning hotter with each thrust of his hips, with each progressively deeper penetration. She rose and rose, straining higher, higher, until her body burst into spasms of something akin to heaven.

She cried out again when she heard Ross's cry. She felt the tightness of his muscles, the pumping of his hips, then, joy, a grand pulsing inside her. He held her as tightly as she held him, and there was joy in that, too.

For what seemed a glorious forever, they lay that way. Finally, his body damp, he slid out to lie beside her. The night air was broken by ragged breathing, both his and hers.

Chloe lay stunned. Then, suddenly and inexplicably, she was overcome. Pressing her cheek against Ross's drumming heart, she began to cry.

In a frightened voice, he asked, "What, princess?"

"Just hold me. Hold me tight."

He gathered her to him as though she were the most precious thing in the world, and held her while she cried. She couldn't explain why she did it, and he didn't ask. He simply held her, stroked her back, whispered sweet nothings of comfort and support against the top of her head.

Gradually her eyes dried and her pulse grew

steadier. "I'm sorry. I don't know what came over me."

"How do you feel now?"

"Better." She took a last jagged breath and rubbed her cheek against his chest. "Satisfied." She thought about that and finally tipped up her head. "I actually feel great. That was the most beautiful—" Her words died when her throat constricted again.

Ross turned them so that they lay on their sides, facing one another. He traced the slim lines of her cheek and jaw, then ran the tips of his fingers down her neck to her collarbone.

Chloe felt a stirring inside. She must have looked startled, because he laughed.

"Didn't think you could feel it again so soon?" When he slid a leg between hers, she moved against it, but he didn't tease her. He was suddenly serious. "It was beautiful, princess. Even more so than before. I've lived all these years wondering whether I had imagined it. I tried for it over and over. And here, in one shot, you've done it again, and more."

"Not me. Us." She touched him lower.

He gasped. "You're gonna do it again," he said and kissed her.

This time was slower, more leisurely. Ross was the connoisseur, showing Chloe how to tease and withhold, playing the martyr when she did. She took delight in learning the nuances of holding, caressing, leading him to the brink, staying there, and, incredibly, the force of the passion was even greater. This time, when it was done, there were no tears. Eyes closed, she nestled against him, replete and happy. She didn't have a care in the world.

Oblivious to the steady rain that beat down on the roof of the house, they slept. Their twined bodies offered warmth, the soft rug offered comfort. It was nearly four in the morning when Ross gently woke her.

"Let's go upstairs," he whispered, kissing her ear.

Groggy and disoriented, she reached for him. "What is it?"

He was on his knees, gathering her into his arms. "Nothing. I just want to take you to bed."

"You're not leaving?" Her arms tightened around his neck, but he chuckled.

"I want to take you in bed—"

"Are you . . . again?"

"Shhh. I want to be able to remember what your bed feels like, for all those long lonely nights ahead," he drawled. He crossed the living room and took the stairs with her in his arms and a minimum of effort. "I want you to be haunted the same way," he added, less humorous now. "You'll lie in your bed and remember the feel of me until you're ready to burst."

Fully awakened, Chloe was warm all over. Her breast was snug to his chest, her hip nestled against his naked belly. It was still night. Under cover of darkness, she could do anything. Her lips turned recklessly to his shoulder, her tongue moistening a spot, her teeth leaving a mark.

"Heeeey! Watch that!" He put her down, letting her slide slowly over the length of him. His hand stayed at the small of her back, pressing her against a full erection. To Chloe's amazement, she was just as aroused.

Their lips met, open now and sure. There was no limit to this pleasure, only the need for more and more.

"The bed," she croaked in haste, tearing herself away to pull back the quilt. She fell onto the sheets with him, and there was a fury to this union, a blend of yearning, fear, and unbridled greed. Morning was coming. They couldn't get enough of each other. When they finally climaxed and collapsed, their bodies were slick and exhausted. Again they slept.

When Chloe opened her eyes next, it was to the gray light of a soggy morning and, more brightly, to Ross. His dark hair was disheveled. He was staring down at her.

Breaking into a smile, he said, "I wanted to see if it would work."

"See if what would work?"

"If I could wake you up by willing it. I've been sending brain waves."

"Brain waves didn't wake me." She yawned. "I'd have woken anyway."

He stretched and grimaced. "I feel well used."

"That's one way to put it," she said, but she was thinking ahead. How not to? Morning was here.

She rolled away, but he rolled her right back and held her in place with an arm on either side. "Don't. After last night you can't turn away."

"Can't?"

"Won't. Let's talk," he said gently and sat up. His eyes wandered to her hair, which was spread on the pillow, then the sheets, which bunched at her navel. He looked at everything in between as though it were priceless. At last, in a deep voice, he said, "I love you, Chloe."

She reached to cover his mouth, not ready for that, but he caught her hand and pinned it to the pillow. Leaning down, he gave her a long, silencing kiss. When his mouth left hers again, he said, "I love you and want to marry you."

She shook her head.

"I do," he insisted.

Her heart ached. She wasn't ready, wasn't ready

at all. "Last night we made love. Saying 'I love you' is something else entirely."

Ross didn't budge. "Argue as much as you want, but you won't change this. I love you. I wish I could say that I loved you eleven years ago—it would all sound romantic. I wanted you then. I knew that there was something in you—deep in you—that intrigued me. But I didn't get to know you. A few hours is too short a time."

"It's hardly been much more than that now," she protested.

"It's been more than two weeks."

"It's been less than two days."

"Tell me you didn't think of me."

She recalled those long hours after New Hampshire. "I can't. I thought of you. But in order to love a person you have to spend time with that person."

"You're clutching at straws. I love you. If you were honest with yourself, you'd tell me that you love me, too."

That was what she feared most. There was no place in her life for that kind of love. "You don't know what I feel."

"I know what I felt last night. You couldn't have faked your reactions. Sorry, Chloe, but you responded out of love. That's all there is to it."

"No. Not all." She needed time. She knew what she had to say. "I responded to you out of need.

Call it lust or physical desire, but don't call it love."

"You're afraid," he announced.

There was a deathly silence. The air pulsed between them.

"You're afraid to let go of the past," he went on. "It's so much a part of you that you're terrified to live without it."

"That's not true," she cried.

"Then why don't you try? You did it for a night—why not for a week? A month? A year?" He softened. "I'm not asking you to renounce your past, just to accept it and move on." He paused, suddenly a shade unsure. "You did enjoy last night, didn't you?"

"Oh, yes," she breathed so quickly that her words stopped dead for lack of a follow-up.

His smile filled the gap. It was a full, warm curve of the firm lips that had given her such pleasure through the night. His gaze dropped to her breasts, then her bare middle. When he bent to kiss her navel, she clutched his hair. But to push him away? Or to hold him there? Lord, she didn't know.

After a night of beauty, the morning was dreary and dark. After a night of clear-cut emotions, the new day's emotions were muddy and dense. She needed time, needed space. Turning her face into the pillow, she let her hands slowly slide from his hair.

"I want you to work for me, Chloe."

Her eyes shot back to his. "Work for you? How can I do that? I have my own business."

He brushed a tendril of hair from her cheek. "I mean, I want to retain your firm."

She was startled. She hadn't considered this twist. "For what?"

"To cater our board meetings," he drawled facetiously. "Come on, you know what you do. I'd like to hire ESE as a geological consultant, starting with a set of revised plans for the Rye Beach Complex."

Business, then? Suddenly self-conscious, Chloe drew the sheet to her armpits and sat up. She forced a feeble smile. "So it's bribery now? You'd try to hook my business, then slowly reel me in?"

"If necessary." His grin came and went. "I've toyed with the idea all week. It was what I wanted to discuss when I arrived Friday. What do you think? Will you do it?"

"No."

"Why not? It's a good business move."

"Actually," she thought aloud, "you're right. It is a good business move. I'll do it, but only if Lee handles the work."

"I don't want Lee."

She had never doubted it. "That's why I can't do this. Can you imagine us trying to work together? After last night? I'm not sure how much work we'd get done."

He sighed. "At least you don't deny that."

"I never did. I just don't know how much more there is to it than that." But she lied. Making love with Ross was as close, as deep, as merged as she had ever been with another person, and that included Crystal, which was saying a lot. She would always be attracted to Ross, would always feel that special connection.

Sadly, she slipped out of bed and stood at the window. She felt as lonely, as dismal as the day. Was the pain of separating from Ross worth the joy of being with him? Was the pain her punishment for self-indulgence?

She heard his footsteps behind her and sighed when he circled her waist and drew her back against him. For another minute, no more, she would savor it. Another minute, that was all.

"I have to leave this morning," he said softly.

"This morning?"

"I have a date in New York."

"A date." That stopped her. "Business or pleasure?"

"Pleasure."

She turned. "You just told me you loved me."

"I love her, too."

The mischief in his eyes tipped her off. "Your mom."

"Smart girl," he said with a smile.

Chloe was inordinately pleased. "I didn't realize she lived in New York."

"She doesn't. She's visiting."

"And you left her for the weekend?"

"With pleasure." And he showed no sign of guilt. "My mother has never been the easiest woman to get along with. And the fact that I loaned her my place pleased her more than my company would have. But I promised to take her to an opening at an art gallery she sponsors." He cleared his throat. "She's on another of her infamous culture kicks."

Chloe couldn't help but grin. "Like the violin lessons?"

"Like the violin lessons."

Their eyes shared amusement, but it faded fast. In its place was raw desire, back with a vengeance.

"Ahhh, Chloe," Ross murmured and caught her lips.

She tried to turn away. "It's too late." She turned back again, needy. She kissed him, then breathed, "We have to stop. Really, we do."

But she wanted him too much for that. He backed her to the bed and followed her down, and she met him willingly. When he was gone, there would be soul-searching aplenty. But not now. Not yet.

8

Her soul-searching began the instant the brown BMW pulled from her drive and disappeared from sight.

"I'll be in touch, princess," he had said when he kissed her good-bye.

"You shouldn't, Ross," she had said, though her throat was tight with emotion. "It's better this way."

He hadn't said anything more, had simply turned on his heel and walked off.

The sense of loss she had felt then should have eased as the day wore on, but it didn't. It grew sharper, forcing her to a deeper level of soul-searching. On this level she felt great guilt. Twice, now, she had been with Ross. Had it not been for the first time, Crystal might still be alive.

The pain of her memory of that time was so great that she rarely went there. Now she did. She and Crystal had double-dated that rainy Saturday night and had returned home on a sour note, largely from Chloe's distraction. When Crystal confronted her, Chloe told her about Ross. She hadn't meant to gloat, only to share the excitement.

But Crystal was furious. Hurt, jealousy, anger— Chloe had never been able to sort through her twin's rage. Crystal had run from the house, taken her small sports car, and sped away. Within an hour the police were at the door to report that the small car had skidded on the wet road and slammed into a tree. Crystal had died instantly.

Chloe twitched. Her forehead was bathed in sweat. Throwing an arm over her eyes, she sank more deeply into the sofa. For years she had lived with the guilt of causing Crystal's death.

But there was new guilt now. Ross had fallen in love with her and she had allowed it to happen. Since she couldn't marry him, he would be hurt, which was the last thing she wanted. He deserved the best, the finest. He deserved a wife and children and all those things she might have wanted herself, had life been different. Causing him pain increased her own pain ten-fold. Because, when all was said and done, she loved him, too.

That was the deepest layer unearthed in her soul-search. She did love Ross, but it had no future. There would always be yesterday and the ghosts she lived with. Ross had stolen her heart, but only a part. The rest had either died with Crystal, or died a little more each time she saw the grief on her parents' faces. Ross deserved a whole-hearted woman. She wanted that for him.

After developing a throbbing migraine, Chloe was in bed by eight, and there was pain beyond her head. Ross's scent clung to her sheets, the remembered feel of his body seared her skin. She burned inside, with no outlet.

In time she fell asleep. After two nights without, it was deep and mercifully uninterrupted. She woke up only when Lee hollered from the foot of the stairs, "Chloe? Rise and shine!"

She yawned, stretched, remembered and felt pain, then relief. Lee often woke her with a yell. This wouldn't be the last time. Life would go on without Ross. Yes, it would.

Climbing from bed, she showered, dressed, neatened the room and joined Lee for breakfast.

"Good weekend, kid?" he asked around a mouthful of toast.

"Not bad."

"So what happened?"

"Nothing."

"He didn't sleep at my place Saturday night, Chloe."

She helped herself to coffee. "How do you know

he stayed over Saturday night? How do you know he didn't go back to New York?"

"His car was here Sunday morning."

She couldn't begrudge him the gentle teasing. He was a dear friend. "You're getting snoopy in your old age."

"I live right next door. How could I miss it?"

"You could have looked the other way."

"And pass up the pleasure of seeing you blush? You don't do it very often, you know."

With determined steadiness she sipped her coffee. "I'm not doing it now. What you see is the freshness of morning—"

"—made fresher by a stimulating weekend."

"Stimulating," she said with a grunt. "That's one word for it."

"He's a good man, Chloe. I liked him."

"He liked you, too. The two of you aren't all that different."

"Maybe because we care about you."

Chloe smiled. "You're sweet." She changed the subject. "When do you leave for Washington?"

"Hold on, pretty lady. I'm still curious. You and that guy had a thing going once. Is it on again?"

Quietly, she said, "I never talked about 'a thing' with Ross. I said I knew him and that whatever might have been between us was over. Don't read something into it that isn't there."

"You make a nice pair."

"It's not your affair."

Lee backed off. "You're right. It's not. If I had any sense I'd marry you myself."

Chloe was suddenly cross. "I wouldn't say yes to you, either!"

"So he did ask you." Her partner smiled. "Fast worker, that one."

Unable to come up with a suitably indignant retort, she stood up with her mug and made to flee to her office.

"What about breakfast?" Lee's voice trailed after her.

"I'm not hungry!"

"You shouldn't work on an empty stomach."

Ross had said the same thing Saturday.

"I'll live!" she shouted over her shoulder and closed the office door.

The telephone jangled, a merciful reminder of the workday ahead. It was Alabama. Had she made a decision on handling the study for the citizens' group in Mobile? No. She hadn't even thought about it once during the weekend. It would mean a week on location taking samples of Gulf water and testing the ocean floor composition. It was a potentially fascinating project, since the toxic waste burning plan was so new.

"Yes, Ms. Farwell. I'll take the job. What's the exact status of the waste burning now?"

A gentle voice responded with concern. "The

tanker will be leaving Mobile two weeks from tomorrow loaded with oil contaminated with PCBs. Those PCBs are cancer-causing. The company that owns the freighter claims that by the time the oil is completely burned, any toxic acid emitted in the smoke will have been neutralized by the seawater. We doubt that."

Chloe made notes as the woman talked. "Where do they plan to do the burning?"

The woman knew her facts and offered them up, along with a detailed list of the equipment Chloe would need. She also advised Chloe on making arrangements with the local university for the use of their lab.

Hanging up the phone, Chloe was pleased. With the use of a lab, she would be able to spend evenings analyzing the samples she collected. Four or five days out, and the job would be done.

The project was exciting. More than that, the escape from Little Compton was just what she needed. It would give her a head start at putting Ross out of her mind.

Her pencil moved over the paper, making further notes on the Alabama project. She would fly down in three weeks, by which time the tanker would have reached its proposed burn site and started to work. Three weeks would take her into the second week in November. After a week in Mobile, Thanksgiving would be at hand.

Thanksgiving. She felt a soft, distant shudder. Should she go home? Alabama was in the vicinity of Louisiana. Mobile was a hop, skip, and jump from New Orleans. She hadn't seen her parents in a long time. She missed them a lot. Same with her brothers. One of them might be there, too.

But there would be memories of another Thanksgiving, not only in Chloe's mind but in those of her parents and brothers. Could she face those? In eleven years she had never made it home for Thanksgiving. They must have guessed why. No doubt they were relieved. Looking at Chloe was seeing Crystal, too. She hated to impose that on a family Thanksgiving.

The phone rang again. "Chloe? Howard Wolschinski here. I just got a call from Stephenson. He's ready to talk." He paused. Chloe didn't know what to say. "Are you still there?" he asked.

"I'm here, Howard." She sighed, resigned. She should have known. "That's good news," she said with forced enthusiasm. "Has he given on all of our points?"

"He hasn't given on anything yet. But he says that he hears what you're saying and is willing to have you work with his people to revise the plans."

"That's fine. My studies and findings are all clearly outlined in the report I did for you. I'll have one of my assistants give him a call."

"He wants you."

"Did he say that?"

"Loud and clear. His exact words were, 'If it were anyone else, I'd have doubts. But Chloe Mac-Daniel has a spirit that can convince the men of the Hansen Corporation that they'd be dumb not to follow her advice.' I wrote it right down, Chloe. Thought you'd be pleased."

"Oh, yeah," she murmured under her breath. The snake. He'd stolen her own words.

"What was that?" Howard asked.

"Ah, nothing, Howard. Just a thought." She cleared her throat. "Are you sure he won't settle for another member of the firm?"

"I doubt it. You'll work with him, won't you, Chloe. I told him you would."

"Howard, how can you do this to me? Why can't you convince him that another member of the firm—even Lee, my partner—will do just as well?"

"I suppose I could try if I wanted to."

"But you don't."

"No."

"You just lost my vote."

Howard laughed roundly. "Thank goodness you don't live up here. You'd have the whole district against me. Seriously, though, we have to get moving on this. The referendum is scheduled for early November. Ross wants to meet with you A-S-A-P so that his team can get to work on some changes."

"A-S-A-P. When is that?"

"Yesterday."

I met with him yesterday, she thought. "I can't make it before Wednesday, Howard." It was just another job, she told herself. Just another job.

"Wednesday will be fine."

"Should I meet them up at the site?" One place would be as bad as the next. But if there were others around, the temptation would be less.

Howard dashed her hopes. "He wants you in New York. That's where the drawing boards are. He'll make arrangements for your transportation and housing. I have to get back to him later to tell him when. Wednesday, you say?"

She gave a low but very audible drawn-out sigh. "It's as good a day as any."

"That's my girl! I'll call you with the details. Okay?"

"You're the boss."

She should have felt victorious, hanging up the phone. If Ross caved in, there would be no need for a referendum and the Rye Beach Complex would be built on an environmentally sound plan. How much better could things be?

Tossing her hair over her shoulder, she grabbed her now empty mug and stomped through the living room into the kitchen, where she poured more coffee and reached for the sticky bun Lee had left. That was when she spotted the open door to his office.

"Lee!" She burst in, rousing her partner from the depths of a thick folder. "Lee, you're just the person I need." So much for gentlemen's agreements. Despite what she'd told Howard, if Lee would fill in for her, she would send him to New York. She could play just as dirty as Ross.

"Umm?"

"I need you to fill in for me in New York on Wednesday. Can you make it?"

He was shaking his head before she'd even finished. "I'll be in Washington. Why? A problem?"

"No. Nothing much." She mumbled the last and turned away.

"Chloe. Get back here. You'd never rush in asking me to fill in for you for nothing much." A look came over his face. "Oh." He cleared his throat. "So he called you, too."

She frowned. "Howard called you?"

"Ross called me. I think his offer is good."

"Offer? Ross? What are you talking about?"

It was Lee's turn to frown. "I'm talking about the phone call I received from Ross Stephenson no more than a half hour ago. He wants to retain our services. What are you talking about?"

A furious Chloe leaned on Lee's desk. "I already refused him! I'm talking about the phone call from Howard Wolschinski saying that Ross is ready to revise the Rye Beach proposal."

"That's great!"

"It's not! He wants me to work with him and that's the last thing I want to do!"

Lee was suddenly very gentle and very serious. He pointed her into a chair and rounded the desk to make sure that she sat. Perching nearby, he said, "Okay, pretty lady. Tell me about it."

She felt utterly helpless. "Ross is willing to make the changes, but he refuses to go by my report. He wants me to work with his people, in person, in New York."

"I gather," he said, stroking his beard, "that you aren't bothered by New York, per se."

"You gather correctly."

"Chloe, what's wrong?" he asked softly. "The man seems intelligent and honest. You shouldn't have any problem. You can be in and out of the city in no time."

At wit's end, she said, "He thinks he's in love with me, that's the problem. If it were only a matter of business, I wouldn't worry. But Ross says he wants to marry me."

"So what's the problem?"

"I can't marry him." She pleaded for his understanding. "And I'm not sure I can take his constant pressure."

"Are you afraid you might give in?" He erased the question with a wave. "Backtrack. Why can't you marry him? You're free."

"Not quite."

"You're not making sense, pretty lady. From what I can see, there's nothing in the world to keep you from marrying Ross."

"What if I don't love him?" she blurted out.

"If you don't love him, then you're right to hold out. And if you don't love him, you'll have no trouble putting him off. He'll get tired after a while." Lee was watching her face very, very closely. "That's not the real problem, is it? You do love him."

She blew out a breath, turning it into a sigh, and looked at the ceiling. "I suppose. But I can't marry him. Being with him can only be painful for both of us."

"If he believed that, he wouldn't be asking to work with you."

She grunted. "So why did he call you?"

"He wants to retain us as consultants. Did you actually say that you refused him?"

"Yes. He brought it up yesterday morning before he left."

"But it's what we need, Chloe. You mentioned trying to get corporate work when we talked on Saturday. The timing couldn't be better."

She eyed him sharply. "Did you say something to him while he was here? Did you tell him we were looking for new business?" She didn't want Ross's pity, or his charity.

"I did not! For one thing, I didn't have a minute

alone with the man from the time I left here Friday night. You monopolized him."

She snorted and looked away. "He's as sneaky as they come."

"That's no way to talk about the man who loves you."

"Lee, puleeze."

He held up a hand. "Okay. I won't tease. This isn't teasing stuff. He'll pay a monthly retainer as an advance on services rendered. If we work more, we bill him for the overage. If we work less, we keep the retainer. It couldn't be better."

That didn't surprise Chloe. Ross might be a rat, a snake, and a fox, but he wasn't a thief.

"The work is right up our alley," Lee was saying. "The Hansen Corporation is involved in dozens of different projects at any given time. There'd be variety and involvement in important issues—"

"You're right, Lee," she cut in. "I can't argue. The logic of this is perfect. By all means, accept his proposal, as long as you work with him." She said the last with a touch of venom. She was being pushed into a corner, and was striking out at the only person in sight.

"He'd be hiring the firm, Chloe. I might be working on one project, you might be called for the next."

"I don't think I can do that on a continuing basis. It'd be too painful. You can work for him. I won't."

"But your area of expertise is different from mine."

"My mind is made up."

Surprisingly, there was little tension in the silence that followed. Chloe wanted to think that her outburst had cleared the air. At least, she'd been honest. Lee knew how she felt.

"You know, Chloe," he said, sitting straighter. "You were right the other day when we talked. I don't know everything about you—all those little secrets you keep bottled up inside. I didn't even know so many existed until this business with Ross." He grew beseechful. "But you have to work out whatever it is that's bothering you. Hell, you should be with him, Chloe. He loves you, you love him. Do you have any idea how many marriages are based on much less?" Lee had been married. He knew this first-hand.

"But a man like Ross deserves more than I can give him."

Lee tossed a hand in the air. "That's a bunch of crap, and you know it. If you want him, you can work out the kinks that hang you up." He rose and went to the window, stared out, turned back. "Damn it, Chloe, you have so much going for you. Are you going to sit back and let some great mystery from the past ruin your future? I thought you were a doer! You wouldn't be where you are today if you didn't believe in working for what you believe in."

Chloe couldn't say a thing. Lee had never talked to her this way before. If another man had said what he had, she would have ignored him. But she couldn't ignore Lee. She respected his opinion too much.

The horrified look on his face said that he hadn't planned the outburst. He softened. "Hey, I'm sorry. I came across a little too strong." He paused. "But I meant what I said. Either you can let it continue to get you down or you can fight it." He thrust the long fingers of one hand through his hair. "Ach, I don't even know what it is. But I believe that you can overcome whatever. I don't know what you were before, Chloe, but you're a strong woman now. Don't let a good thing escape."

She smiled sadly. "You don't understand."

"No. I don't." He sighed. "What say we drop it for a while?" At her nod, he added a final thought. "But promise me that if you want to talk, you'll come to me? I have broad shoulders."

She stood and gave him a hug. "Thanks, Lee. I appreciate that." Stepping back, she looked up at him. Funny, he was warm and strong and in his way as good-looking as Ross, but she felt no desire, no great inner spark.

Lee held out a hand. "Friends?"

She met his hand. "Friends."

"And we'll accept the offer from Stephenson?"

She yanked her hand back. "No. Yes. I don't

know." She strode toward the door. "Do what you want!"

How to go from high to low in seconds, she mused, as she returned to her office and settled in at the desk. Ross was forcing her hand, totally determined. What was it he had said about love being wanting and wanting until one would do nearly anything?

She did have options. She could stand firm and refuse to have anything to do with Ross, send someone to New York in her place for the Rye Beach negotiations, systematically shuttle retainer work to another member of the firm.

Another option was more dangerous. She could go to New York and do his work, remaining neutral. Did she have a chance in hell of doing that?

Lee's words returned with frightening clarity. Did she love Ross enough to fight herself—and her past—for him? Could she go back to New Orleans and face the ghosts, finally put them to rest?

She hit emotional overload with that last thought. Too much had happened too fast. She couldn't think about it anymore. There was work to be done—if she was to be en route to New York by Wednesday.

With a long steadying breath, she sorted through the papers before her. There were people to call, meetings to set up, reports to plan out before she left, and the rush was for the best. Her mind would be filled. Worrying was useless. Only time would give her the answers she needed.

Unfortunately, Ross wasn't as patient, but he received a different Chloe on the phone that afternoon, a more subdued one. She recognized his voice immediately, had been half expecting to hear it. Its sound sent a ripple through her, but it died quickly. She was exhausted.

"How are you?" he asked.

"I'm fine."

"It's good to hear your voice. I miss you."

"You've been gone barely twenty-four hours."

"You've been counting, have you?"

She hadn't. Well, maybe she had. But she wasn't about to admit it. "I'm counting now. I have five different reports to go through this afternoon, not to mention phone calls, proposals, and what-have-you. It seems I have a rush job in New York. Some snotty executive thinks his work is the only thing that counts."

"I can see you got up on the wrong side of the bed. Bad morning?"

"Busy."

"Anything interesting?"

"Uh-huh."

He sighed. "Ah. We're pulling teeth again."

"No. There's just nothing I feel like discussing."

With you, she might have added. He had intruded on her life far too much.

"You sound down." He sounded concerned. "Is something wrong?"

"I'll be fine." But she wondered. Much as she fought it, the sound of Ross's voice affected her.

"What is it, Chloe? Please tell me. Something's bothering you. I can hear it in your voice. Your spirit's gone." He paused. When she said nothing, he said, "I'm driving up."

"No! I'm okay. Really. I'm tired. That's all."

"You have no idea what I feel when I hear that pain in your voice."

"Then why did you do it?" she blurted out.

The silence was long and heavy. Then he sighed. "You've, ah, figured out my messages?"

"You could say that. What I'd like to know is why you had to go behind my back to box me in. Why didn't you call me directly?"

"I mentioned it to you last weekend. You refused. I may be many things, but I'm not a glutton for punishment. That's your specialty." Chloe's gasped, but he went on. "I had no intention of calling you this morning to rehash what I said yesterday. There seemed to be more effective ways of convincing you—"

"—forcing me . . ."

". . . convincing you to work with me. It makes good sense. You're the one familiar with the Rye

Beach proposal and its problems. To bring in someone else would be a waste of time. As for the other—"

"The other is Lee's affair," she cut in. "He's handling any account with the Hansen Corporation. If you want to work with him, be my guest. I can vouch for his credentials and his skill, but I won't be involved."

"Then why are you upset?" he asked a little too calmly. "If Lee will be doing the dealing, it won't affect you."

"Fat chance," she murmured not quite softly enough.

"Ah, ah, princess. Let's have none of that. If you're into soft murmurings, use them to talk about love."

"Ross."

"I love you."

"So you've said." She tried to sound indifferent, but her tone was more of a plea.

"I mean it. That's why I'm doing all this."

"What?" she cried in a facetious show of emotion. "Don't you value my brilliance, my experience, or my expertise in the field?"

"Depends on what field you're referring to," he drawled. "In the field of passion—"

"That wasn't the one I was talking about, and you know it. Why do you twist my words, Ross? Do you like upsetting me?"

He was suddenly sober. "No. I'm trying to goad you into facing your feelings. I love you, Chloe. I want to have you near me, so I manipulated your cooperation. You may not be ready to admit that you need me as much as I need you, but I have no pride. I need you, and I'm not giving you up. Not yet, at any rate."

Chloe listened sadly. He sounded honest and sincere. Maybe he did need her. But what about her needs? "You're rushing me, Ross. I don't know whether I'm coming or going. Please, give me time?"

"You have till Wednesday. I've made arrangements for you to take the nine-fifty train from Providence."

"The train? I'd rather drive. It's more convenient."

"I don't want you driving into the city. Leave your car in Providence. Your ticket will be held there for you and I'll be at the station waiting."

"Ross—"

"It's settled."

Her lips turned down. "That's what I like about you. You're so democratic."

He said a gentle "I love you, too," before hanging up.

9

Ross was indeed waiting at the station when her train pulled in. She had barely stepped onto the platform when he was beside her. He took her bag and her arm in one smooth move. "Have a good trip?" he asked, glancing down as he guided her along.

"It was fine." And she had to admit that there was something fine about being met like this, something that went beyond mere convenience. New York was New York, always a little intimidating. Ross's protectiveness felt good, though she wasn't about to tell him that. "Where are we going?" she asked when he hustled her to a cab, then gave the driver the same Park Avenue address to which she had sent her check.

"I thought you'd like to see Hansen's corporate headquarters. The team working on the Rye Beach Complex won't be meeting until tomorrow, but you might feel more comfortable seeing the layout before you get bogged down in work. I have things to take care of while we're there."

Indeed, he seemed all business. There was no welcome kiss, no hug, not even in the privacy of the cab, and she wasn't complaining. She had felt a jolt seeing him back at the train, and felt tingles even now. She needed all the time she could get to regain full control.

The Hansen Corporation was every bit as impressive as she had known it would be. Ross Stephenson wasn't one to do things halfway. As she toured offices that consumed three full floors, no one she saw was idle.

Her guide was one of the vice presidents, a soft-spoken man whom she instantly liked. Ross himself had disappeared with a soft apology shortly after they arrived. She saw nothing of him until late afternoon, when he materialized in the drafting room, where she was admiring the architect's plans for a museum and theater complex in Des Moines.

"What do you think?"

Delight lit her face. "It's wonderful, Ross. You have a brilliant architect. From the looks of the plans, this museum will be a drawing card for all of Iowa."

His smile held satisfaction. "That's what we're hoping. Any suggestions?"

She grinned. "You mean, will I now go on and pick the thing to bits on the geological score?"

"Something like that."

"I have no way of knowing about this particular project. Looking at the designs, I can mention potential sources of worry—drain pipes, for instance—but unless I know something about the land there, I can't offer constructive criticism."

When Ross put his lips by her ear, she realized that it was the nearest he'd come since she arrived. The warmth of his skin by her cheek sent a tingle through her. "Thank God for that," he said in a stage whisper, though they were alone in the room. He straightened. "The day's pretty much over. Let's get going."

Chloe gathered her things. It had been an unexpectedly pleasant and interesting afternoon. If each of her days here were like it, she might survive after all.

But something hung heavy in a half-hidden corner of her mind. It had New Orleans written all over it. After New York, there would be Rhode Island, then Alabama. Should she do New Orleans after that? Would it solve anything? Would it change her feelings for Ross?

No doubt, she did love him. Walking down a long corridor with him now, she felt like a princess. He ruled the place, but he was gentle and caring. He loved her. Was she worthy of that?

They were silent during the cab ride to Ross's brownstone. "You'll be staying here," he told her calmly, breaking what was almost a truce.

"Ohhhh, no," she balked, but followed him out

of the cab. "I'll go to a hotel. The city is full of them. You can go inside and make a call to book the room that should have been booked on Monday."

Ross led her up the front stairs to the tall oak door, turned the key in the lock, and let them in. Once inside the gracious hall, he took her coat. "There are three floors here. I sleep on the second. You can have the third all to yourself. I'm not suggesting that you sleep with me, only that you stay here. It'll be more convenient."

Chloe recalled what he had said on the phone about needing her near him. Separate bedrooms? On separate floors?

Remembering Rye Beach and feeling suddenly lighter, she said, "Okay. I'll take the penthouse." She had taken the penthouse in Rye Beach, too. They shared that past, and a grin of remembrance now.

"Come," he said warmly. "I'll show you around."

From first to second to third floor they went, examining furniture, artwork, and memorabilia from his travels. No room in the house would have won a designer's award, yet every room had a warmth that reached out to Chloe and made her feel at home.

Ross, too, made her feel at home. He put no pressure on her, so she put none on herself. They ate at a nearby restaurant, then returned for a quiet evening of reading. When Chloe excused herself shortly after eleven, he bid her good night with a noticeable lack of lechery.

"You'll find an extra blanket in the closet. If you want more towels check the cupboard in the bathroom." He looked up from his papers, but didn't rise.

"I'll be fine." She smiled. "Good night."

"Good night. Sleep well."

One glance back as she left the room told her that he had returned to his papers. She took the stairs slowly, one flight to the next. This was a side of Ross she had never seen. In the past their relationship had been shaped by physical attraction. Now Ross seemed either immune, or holding his interest in check.

Whichever, she was grateful. Living with him, working with him could have been a nightmare. As it was, she was aware of the fact that he would be sleeping one short flight away. More than once that night she held her breath, hearing a sound, wondering if he was making the climb.

Her bedroom door remained closed, and when she fell asleep, she slept well.

It was good. Thursday and Friday were packed with work, long hours spent huddled with the masterminds of the Rye Beach Complex. They were amenable to her suggestions, often mildly questioning, sometimes strongly doubting, but always ready to listen. Ross was absent during most of the work, dropping in to check on the progress, but otherwise yielding to the men beneath him.

Chloe asked him about it Friday evening. "I thought you'd be more comfortable if I kept my distance at the office," he said.

"But aren't you concerned about the project? For all you know the revised plans may be unacceptable to you personally."

"I doubt that," he replied, smiling comfortably. "I trust you. And I trust the men you're working with. They know what I want." He paused, eyes changing, voice lowering. "So do you."

Her throat grew tight. It was the first thing he had done that was at all suggestive. For that reason, she indulged him the lapse. And because the lapse was brief, she let him bribe her to stay in New York until Sunday with a pair of choice tickets to the Big Apple's newest hit musical.

"How did you ever get seats?" she asked in excitement, reaching for the telltale envelope. Ross only raised it much higher, out of reach.

"I have ways." He laughed. "You haven't seen it, have you?"

"You know I haven't! It only opened last week, and you've known every one of my comings and goings since then."

He smiled smugly and changed the subject, but Chloe easily acclimated herself to a Sunday return to Rhode Island. When he announced that he had work to do at the office on Saturday morning, she binged on Fifth Avenue, treating herself to a new dress, shoes, and a purse. Again, though, there was that dark tugging at the back of her mind. The outfit was for New Orleans. If she went, she wanted her parents to be proud. *If* she went.

Saturday afternoon was something else. Had she planned a few hours in the city, they couldn't have been as exciting as the ones Ross planned. From museum to park to ice cream parlor and back, it was a dream time. He was intellectually stimulating and wonderfully adventurous, even-tempered to a fault.

He appeared to be surviving abstinence with no problem but a tic in his jaw. She noticed it when they were the closest—standing side by side before a Calder mobile at the Guggenheim, walking hip to hip through the squeeze of the crowd at Rockefeller Center, sitting knee to knee at a small table in a quiet restaurant.

At least, she wanted to think the tic was from that. She wanted to think he was feeling the strain, because she certainly was. His hands-off policy made working easier, but it did nothing for the desire she felt. It grew through all of Saturday, all of Saturday evening, all of Saturday night. By the time they returned from the theater in the early hours of Sunday morning it was near to bursting.

She took his lead and put it on ice. In the living

room for a nightcap, their conversation was as soft and pleasing as the entire four-day stretch had been. She felt happy. Then she went upstairs, alone, to the bedroom that had been lonely all week, and the ice melted. She dozed and woke, shifting in bed with little hope of relief from frustration. She tried to think of other things, but Ross kept her restless and aching. It was dawn when she finally crept from bed and went to the window.

The city was rising. The deep purples and blues of night were beginning to fade to lighter hues. The tallest of the skyscrapers to the east wore the first pink traces of the sun on its uppermost windows. It was lovely and peaceful. Only the dull ache inside her marred it.

"I couldn't sleep," came a voice at the door. She turned to find Ross standing there. Standing tall, his features hidden in the shadows, he wore a robe that wrapped at the waist and hung to his knees. The unruly rumpling of his hair gave truth to his words. "How 'bout you?"

Her throat was tight. "The same."

She watched him slowly approach. Each step brought him closer to the window, until his features were clear in it. Though his eyes reflected her own torment, he touched her cheek with a tenderness that made her want to weep. She couldn't pull away. She was desperate for his love.

If there were germs of reason floating around,

they vanished with his first kiss. What remained was a hunger that had been days in building. Chloe gave herself up to it without a thought.

Ross touched her everywhere, caressing her through the thin lavender gown, and she touched him right back. But his robe was thick, and she grew impatient. The robe was easily opened and his body bared. She touched him then, bringing low sounds from his throat, and the feeling of power was heady. He began to shake under her stroking. His penis grew thick and engorged.

Moments later, her gown fell to the ground with his robe. His mouth ate at hers, as he lifted her and carried her to the bed. The weight of his body pinned her to the sheets, but there was no pain in it for Chloe. She welcomed his force, wanting even more.

"Yes!" she cried, clutching at his hips to pull him closer.

But Ross tensed at the sound of her voice. He was breathing hard, pressing his forehead to the pillow by her ear. She felt him rock hard and large against her, but he didn't enter.

"I swore I wouldn't do this," he whispered hoarsely, "swore I'd keep my hands off you. I've tried. God knows, I've tried!"

When he raised himself to look at her, his expression shocked her into awareness. "Don't go!" she cried.

"I have to. For this one release, I'd be buying a huge packet of pain."

"No!" Her fingers tightened on his shoulders until her knuckles turned white. She was close to panic. "Please, Ross. I've never asked you for anything else. But please . . . now . . . I can't bear it!"

The impetus was hers, lips and arms and hips all working against him until he surrendered with a moan. Falling to the bed and rolling to his back, he drew her over him, and she loved him that way. She couldn't say the words he wanted to hear, but her body could show him what she felt.

It did that, and quite well. By the time the sun's golden rays breached the windowsill and glistened on their sweat, they were totally spent.

Rasping breaths broke the air, but otherwise, all was quiet. Something was wrong. Chloe felt it the instant her pulse began to slow. There was no talk. No closeness. The satisfaction that usually kept them warm and entwined faded fast.

Ross rose from the bed, retrieved his robe, and left the room. Alone again, Chloe curled into a tight ball with the covers pulled to her ears.

Apparently, it was time to put up or shut up. Ross couldn't live with half-measures—but then, had she really thought he would? Her body might love him to bits, but if she couldn't love the rest with her head and her heart, there was no hope.

She heard the front door slam shortly after he

left her room. She didn't know where he went, and he was back in time to take her to the train station, but even the short ride there was awkward. It wasn't until she was about to board the train that he said more than a full sentence, and then his voice was quiet.

"I'd like to follow through with the liaison between Hansen and ESE, but I think Lee should handle the account. You're right. It'll be too difficult any other way, at least for now."

Chloe wanted to argue, but no words came out.

His eyes held defeat when he looked at her a final time. "I'll be here, Chloe. When you're free, let me know."

On the Saturday after Thanksgiving, Chloe boarded a plane. It taxied and took off, then climbed into the sky and headed north. New Orleans fell behind. New York was ahead. She was going back to Ross.

She tried to sleep, but was too excited. She ate dinner, she read a magazine, she looked out the window and smiled. Where a haunted woman had been just a few days before, was one with a newborn peace.

She had come a very long way in a very short time, but it hadn't been easy. There were dozens of doubts and seconds thoughts dogging her through Mobile, and added days spent wavering there, then fear and unsureness when she arrived at her parents' home in New Orleans on Thanksgiving morning.

Now, as the plane began its descent, she shook her head in amazement. So many years lost over a misunderstanding. But it was cleared up now. It was better. She would call Ross the minute she landed. He would be totally surprised.

But she was the one in for the surprise. Ross was at the airport to meet her, standing tall and dark and vibrant. In a moment of déjà vu, their eyes met over the crowd. Chloe stopped in awe, knowing that her next steps would be as momentous as the ones she had taken eleven years ago. But she was a woman now and finally free to love. Breathing deeply, she ran forward.

Ross met her halfway and crushed her in his arms, holding her tightly enough, long enough to say what he felt without words.

Chloe owed him the words, though. When she drew back to look up at him, her throat was constricted by the same emotion that brought tears to her eyes. A mouthed "I love you" was the best she could do. It was enough.

His face lightened. His eyes glowed. "Let's go home," he said, and, arm in arm, they did just that.

A short time later, they were in Ross's living room, sitting on the sofa, facing one another. He held her hand tightly, while she tried to put into words everything she had learned in New Orleans.

"It was a tragic comedy of errors," she began. "I had blamed myself for going with you and upsetting Crystal, even for tossing that coin, and I felt so guilty when she died that I withdrew into myself. When my parents couldn't get through to me, they sent me to stay with friends in Newport in the hope that the change of scenery would do me good. I thought that they just didn't want me around to remind them of what had happened, so I stayed away. One misunderstanding after another."

"But it's over?" he asked, so obviously needing reassurance that she lifted a hand to his cheek and kissed him.

"Yes," she breathed. "It's over. I was really worried about my mother for a while there. When she learned what I'd thought all these years, she was beside herself with grief. We spent that whole first night talking, just the two of us." She grew pensive. "I'd never had her all to myself before. There were always the three of us. But Mom was great, even as upset as she was. She explained so many things to me. It helped."

She looked again at Ross. His eyes were warm with understanding, urging her on.

"She talked about having twins, about watching them grow, about knowing their similarities and their differences. She pointed out that if the tables had been turned, and Crystal had had the affair, I'd have reacted differently. In other words," she sighed, sad but hopeful, "Crystal's reaction was part of her personality, just as the guilt I've lived with all these years is part of mine."

"Is?" Ross asked softly.

"Was," she corrected herself, looking directly at him. He couldn't miss the pleading in her gaze. "I'd like to put it behind me now. Will you help?"

Her pulse tripped for a minute until Ross's wide smile sent it racing on. "That's why I'm here."

She frowned. "Why are you here? I mean, how did you know to be at the airport?"

"Your parents."

"You talked with them?"

"Yesterday." He looked pleased with himself. "You were overdue in Little Compton. Lee called me, we plotted your course, and put two and two together. When I realized you'd gone home I knew why. It was all I could do not to join you there. But it was something you had to do, wasn't it?"

She nodded. "I told them about you."

"Lucky you did. It made the explanations simpler." He paused, vaguely playful, vaguely curious. "What, uh, exactly, did you tell them?"

"That you loved me, that I loved you, that you'd asked me to marry you. But I also told them that I had to work things out there with them, to finally accept Crystal's death, if I ever hoped to be as much of a woman as you deserve."

At the last, all playfulness drained from Ross's

face, leaving a vulnerability that was the flip side of his usual strength. His hand trembled slightly when it cupped her face. "Have I told you how much I love you?" he whispered, kissing her eyes, nose, and mouth in turn.

"You'll have forever to tell me," she whispered back.

"Then you'll marry me?"

"Uh-huh."

"Ahhhhh." With the long sigh, he hugged her again. His breath was warm against her ear.

"Tired?"

His neck smelled of him. She shook her head against it. "Nope."

"You're sure?" He tightened an arm around her waist. "It was a long flight."

"I'm not tired." She grinned. "I don't think I'll sleep for hours."

Ross rose from the sofa and held out a hand. Chloe put hers in it and let him draw her up and into his arms.

"I love you, Ross. You know that, don't you?"

"I have for a long time. I'm only glad you can finally say it. You're free, aren't you, princess?"

She sighed, then smiled and said with a touch, just a touch of New Orleans, "I do believe I am."

He laughed out loud and rolled his eyes. Keeping an arm around her to hold her close, he walked her to the stairs and up.